ISBN-13: 9780999860816

shandathewriter.com

shandathewriter@gmail.com

BrownTrez Press

Water in My Hands
A Story of Love, Loss, and Faith

Shanda The Writer

DEDICATION

Thank you, God, for the gift and miracle of writing. I appreciate the love and support, Mommy and Daddy during this writing journey. Aunt Ann, thank you for encouraging me and always showing how proud you were throughout my life. I know you're looking down on me smiling.

1 BLUE LIGHTS

Tiffany stepped out of the shower and took a deep breath. Wrapping herself in a towel, she stood in front of the mirror.

"With God all things are possible," Matthew 19:26 the sticker above the mirror read.

"Lord help me believe it," she whispered while staring at the mirror in a trance.

Tiffany dare not let anyone know that she woke up feeling incompetent every day of her life. How she always wondered if she wore the right outfit or said the right thing to others.

"Girl, I would love to have your life."

This is what she would hear from friends and family alike. There was no need for her to complain, or so they thought.

She graduated from Loyola Law School with honors and made partner at Marsh & Harrison two years ago, but still doubted herself all the time.

In her mind, her failures with men outshined any success she had. The breakup with Michael a few years back was shocking and unexpected.

"I don't think this is going to work out Tiffany."

"But, why?"

"Because I just need to focus on my career. I can't be in a relationship right now."

"I just don't understand. How am I in the way, Michael?"

"Because I'll have to consider you. This isn't easy, but I have to do what's best for me."

"Best for you? What about me?"

"Look, you'll find someone else. I'm sure we can still be friends."

Anderson, her fiancé, showed up right on time. He was her true love and made the breakup with Michael seem so small. It served him right, taking her for granted. Now, she has a man who loves her.

"Oh no. I have 20 minutes," she said as she checked the time on her phone. Holding her towel, she ran into her bedroom.

"I have got to clean out this closet."

There were shoes, purses, and shirts strewn around on the closet floor.

"This'll have to do today."

She chose a black pantsuit and started getting dressed when her phone rang.

"Hello?"

She was overjoyed to hear Anderson's voice.

"Good morning Tiffany."

"Hey, honey. This is pretty early for you. I thought you were an early-rising telemarketer."

Smiling, she said, "You must have me on your mind."

"Yes, I do. I just want to have more time to talk to you," he said.

"Sure. Can I give you a call back in about 15?"

Tiffany hated to get off the phone, but she could call Anderson from the car. She quickly headed out the door grabbing her briefcase and ran to the car.

Connecting her phone to the Bluetooth, she hurriedly dialed Anderson's phone number.

"Hey. I'm calling you back"

There was a slight pause.

"Yea. I just want to discuss this weekend."

His voice sounded flat, totally different.

"Are you okay? You don't sound like yourself. Are you sick?" she asked Anderson. He's usually at work but told her that he took the day off.

Since they planned to leave for Jamaica the next day, he must've decided to stay home to pack and make sure that everything was in order.

"How did directing go on the set yesterday? Were those actors being difficult again?"

Anderson took a deep breath, ignoring her question

"What time do you want me to pick you up from the airport

tomorrow? The flight leaves at 7, so we want to get there early."

Something wasn't right. He had no excitement in his voice the way he used to. It seemed as if discussing the trip was a burden. Like how he sounds when he tells her he has to get his oil changed.

"Ummm, pick me up at 5:45. That will leave plenty of time to go through security, get some breakfast, and relax before our flight."

Tiffany pulled into the parking lot of Marsh & Harrison reaching for her briefcase.

Pausing, she heard laughter in the background. Anderson heard someone in the background to be quiet.

"Who is that Anderson?" Her voice was one of curiosity.

"Tiffany, it's just my workout group. Remember I said I found a workout group on Meetup? I gotta stay fly."

He laughed for what seemed like forever.

"Oh yea, I remember."

Anderson loved working out, but all of his friends were busy in the morning so he decided to find a workout group.

"So I want my pretty lady and wife-to-be to make sure that all of her ducks are in a row."

Tiffany smiled, she loved it when he called her that. There was no reason to doubt Anderson. Men could be just as moody as women, and often he's exhausted from work.

"Baby I gotta go. I'm almost late for this briefing at 8 with my legal team."

He gave her a lecture about getting up on time.

"Alight Tiff. I'll talk to you later. Love you."

 With those three words, her day felt lighter already.
She waited just a moment and said, "I love you more."

As she walked into the building she wondered how she got so lucky. Everything in her life was finally in place.

Anderson was the man she prayed for. Their meeting was one from a romance novel.

After taking the law school exam with a broken heart, she met him at Cajun Seafood. He tapped her on her shoulder.

When she turned around, she saw the most handsome man in the world. Not only did he have a beautiful smile, but she noticed his physique. He worked out.

But, this wasn't the time for that. She needed a break. Entertaining any man right now was not an option for her.

"Excuse me, I know this may be a bit too forward, but what's your name?"

She rolled her eyes. "Tiffany."

He paused. "This is my first time here. Can you tell me what's good?"

"I usually get the blue smoked crab. The boiled crawfish isn't bad either" she replied.

This was not the time for him to try to talk to her. Exhaustion and frustration was what she felt.

She quickly paid for her food and walked towards her favorite table in the corner.

"Umm, excuse me." It was him again. He wanted to know if she was dining alone.

"Yes, I am. You have a lot of courage, huh?" she said with a forced smile.

Pulling out her cell phone, she hoped that he would see that she was preoccupied and walk away.

Anderson sat down without an invitation, which annoyed her even more.

"Do you go to Loyola too?" he asked.

She looked up from her phone. "Yes, law school."

He told her that he was a student at Loyola University studying Fine Arts. His dream was to be a director one day.

"Spike Lee is my idol. He's unique you know?"

As he talked about his dreams and inspirations, his face lit up. Tiffany found herself wanting to know more about him.

"Nobody puts Spike in a box, and he's not afraid to tackle controversial issues."

They both agreed.

"So, what made you want to be a lawyer?" he asked.

"I guess it's because I've seen how biased the legal system could be based on a person's race or economic status. I feel a deep sense of anger when I see two people of different races commit the same crime, but one would receive a harsher punishment because of the color of their skin."

He stared at her in awe and said, "Wow. That's so true. We need an attorney like you in this world."

She smiled at his statement.

"Yea my dad was an attorney, so I know a little bit about the territory. I'll be working for Marsh and Harrison," she said beaming with pride.

They're known for representing defendants in high profile cases, but they often did pro bono work to help those who may not be able to afford their legal representation."

Tiffany looked down at her watch.

"I gotta go. It's been a long day. I enjoyed talking to you, Mr. Anderson."

Before she got up to leave, Anderson stopped her and motioned for her to sit back down. Peering into her eyes with curiosity he asked, "So, do you have a boyfriend?"

Tiffany wondered how many questions he was going to ask her. The conversation grew quiet.

"Well, I'm fresh out of a relationship," she said while moving her food around on her plate.

He sat back in his chair smiling again.

"Well, hopefully, things will turn around soon. You're a beautiful woman, and I hope you'll let a Brutha call you."

She loved the fact that he was the one that approached her first. Usually, it's the other way around.

After they exchanged information and parted ways, there was a feeling deep down in her heart.

"Is he the one?" she asked herself as she walked away.

They were inseparable after that spending whole weekends together, taking trips to the beach, going to plays, and dining at the finest restaurants.

Three years later, he went from working on small, independent projects to now working with A-list actors. His film "The Heart of It" broke box office records last year and was a worldwide success.

When he won his first Oscar, she was right there with him being his biggest cheerleader.

As he stood up to receive his reward, she whispered in his ear, "I'm so proud of you."

She smiled to herself when she thought about how hard he worked. It was a blessing to be a part of his life.

Turning inward, she thought about the dedication and sacrifices she had to make for her own career. Her first case will forever be etched in her mind.

"We the jury find the defendant Sarah Windson innocent of murder in the first degree."

Sarah hugged Tiffany and the rest of her defense team.

The underdog won against the D.A. whose goal was to tear her client apart. It felt good to know that she changed a life and, like Anderson, she was living her dream.

They had three years of stories to tell, and he was her dream come true. Still, things have been tense lately.

"I don't ever see you. Between my cases and you being on set, our relationship isn't being nurtured. Plus, you're always on the road," she said a few days ago.

Anderson grew frustrated. "Tiffany, you know this has always been my dream. Plus, I'm doing this for us, for our future."

"Love my job, but it'll be nice to have a change of scenery" she whispered to herself as she opened the door to the building.

For her, the vacation couldn't come soon enough.

"Hey, baby?" Tiffany said as she came downstairs. Today was the day to get away and she was excited.

"Hey, Tiff. You got everything ready?"

There it was, that dry look and monotone voice.

"He's just tired. It's 5:30 and he's just not used to getting up so early," she thought to herself.

"Why do we have to get to the airport so early? Our flight doesn't leave until 7:30."

There it was again. His negative behavior started to get to her.

"Umm...somebody needs some Starbucks coffee."

She was in a good mood, but the energy she received from Anderson was bringing her down

Anderson frowned and grabbed her luggage, without saying a word.

"You know what Anderson, I've been looking forward to this trip for months. I understand you are exhausted and tired, but so am I. We don't have to go if this is how it's gonna be."

She tried not to raise her voice. Silence.

"Hey Tiff, I'm sorry. It's just the early morning. I'm not a morning person at all. I apologize for upsetting you."

Anderson reached for her hand and pulled her close to him. "Forgive me?" His face softened.

"Let's get going so we can start that vacation we both deserve, huh?

Tiffany shook her head. "Ok, but let's leave our troubles behind and have fun. We don't get to vacation every day."

They both laughed and started to load up the car. Although she was smiling, something still wasn't right. But life is life, and maybe he was secretly going through something.

Anderson peered at the terminals. "Okay, so it says terminal 4 for American Airlines, right?"

"Yep Anderson, according to this app."

Frustrated, they sat in traffic for a bit until they arrived at their terminal.

"I'm gonna drop you off at the terminal, unload the bags, and try to find a parking space in that parking deck over there. Just wait for me, okay?"

Tiffany frowned but didn't question his plans.

"Okay. See you in a bit."

They had an hour and a half before boarding, so they had plenty of time.

After a few minutes, she saw Anderson walk up to the terminal.

They grabbed their luggage and entered the airport. Going through security was their least favorite part of flying, but it had to be done.

"Oh my goodness I'm glad we are done with that mess. I'm so tired of taking off my shoes when going through security."

Anderson shot her a smile.

"I know Tiff. You and those shoes though. Don't worry, your Yves Saint Laurents won't get damaged. Who wears those shoes to the airport anyway?"

Tiffany rolled her eyes in a jokingly manner.

"You never know when the paparazzi will show up."

They chatted for a while about the first thing they would do when they arrive in Jamaica.

Looking in her bag, she realized that she forgot to pack her phone charger. Her battery was almost dead, and she scolded herself for always forgetting to charge it.

"Oh shoot. I forgot my charger. Did you pack an extra one?"

"No, but you could go to that store over there to get one."

"Yea, I know. I hate to have to go into one of these overpriced stores."

She let out a huge sigh and stood up.

"Wanna come with?" Anderson told her that he would stay where he is.

~~~~~~

"Good afternoon passengers. This is the pre-boarding announcement for flight 89B to Jamaica. We are now inviting those passengers with small children, and any passengers requiring special assistance, to begin boarding at this time. Please have your boarding pass and identification ready. Regular boarding will begin in approximately ten minutes. Thank you."

Tiffany took off towards the convenience store and quickly bought her charger. Running towards the boarding area she let out a deep breath.

"I'm back."

Anderson let out a laugh.

"Okay track star. Fortunately, we are in the last boarding group, so you're good."

They found their seats and settled in.

"Gimmie your hand Anderson. You know how nervous I get."

Anderson smiled and squeezed Tiffany's hand. The pilot announced that the flight was about to start, and the stewardesses showed the emergency procedures.

Before they were instructed to put all cell phones on airplane mode, Tiffany saw Anderson smile at his phone, turn it off, and lean back in his seat. As the plane took off, she looked out of the window, closed her eyes and thought to herself, "He let go of my hand."

~~~~~~

"Why do these people keep leaving these stupid flyers in my door?"

She was back home, silent, coldness. On the other hand, she missed her space, and just wanted to go to sleep.

Throwing her keys on the counter, she dragged the luggage behind her and locked the door.

Anger overwhelmed her as Jamaica was a waste of time. She and Anderson argued almost the entire time. They couldn't agree on where to eat, where to go, or how long to stay when they were finally able to agree on something. It was evident that he didn't want to be there, so they cut the vacation short.

The white down comforter on her bed was so welcoming. Without taking off her shoes, she laid down on the bed. It didn't matter to her if the comforter got dirty. Her pure white canvas of life was already starting to dim. It was just a matter of figuring out why.

The heaviness in her chest seemed to deepen, and she just couldn't find a place of rest.

Just when she was about to fall asleep, her phone rang.

"Hey, Anderson."

There was a slight pause.

"Hey, Tiff. What are you doing?"

She frowned. One minute he's being a jerk, and other times he's jolly. Trying to figure it out at the moment used up too much of her brain space.

"Just relaxing. So glad to be off that plane."

"Me too."

"Hey lady, let's go and grab some dinner tonight. How about August's?

"I don't know. Our vacation left me in a bad mood. I didn't enjoy it, and I just don't wanna argue again. Just tired."

"Baby I know. I know that dinner can't compare to a vacation, but I don't want you going to bed upset. Just say you'll come have dinner with me."

Hesitant, Tiffany agreed to go.

"Sure. What time?"

"How's eight sound?"

"That's fine, I'll be ready."

~~~~~~

Tiffany stared at the menu, not even reading it, just thinking.

"Huh?" she was jolted out of her trance.

"Ummm ma'am, drink. What drink would you like to start with?"

Anderson and the waitress stared at her.

Embarrassed, she put on a smile and asked for water with lemon.

"Earth to Tiffany," Anderson said.

"I'm sorry. I was just so hungry that everything looked good."

Anderson looked down at his phone.

"I'll be right back. Nature's calling."

There it goes, that feeling deep in the pit of her stomach. Looking at his phone and suddenly leaving the table made her feel uneasy.

Tiffany waved her hand.

"Go ahead. Handle your business."

The waitress came back to the table and asked, "Are you ready to order?"

Tiffany looked around and turned to the waitress.

"Can you give us a little more time? I'm going to go check on him to make sure he's okay."

The waitress smiled and shook her head with a look of confusion on her face.

Tiffany stood up and walked towards the restrooms. Anger suddenly took over her as she felt embarrassed to be at the table alone for so long.

The hallway with its darkness always puzzled her. It wasn't warm like the restaurant was, and was a bit creepy.

Following the sign down the hall to the right, she heard a voice coming from the men's restroom area and stood still. It was evident that someone was having a heated conversation.

"Look, I'm at dinner right now."

She knew that voice, it was Anderson's.

"I'm not playing games. I told you that I would call you back later. Yes, I love you. I'm just having dinner with her. It doesn't mean anything. Look, I can't just drop my whole day for you. You have to understand that things like this take time.".

Walking away was an option, but her feet wouldn't move. His voice softened.

"Hurt people hurt people. I'm so sorry and I'll call you later."

Anderson got off the phone and started to walk back to his table. He was startled when he saw her step out of the corner.

All Tiffany could do was stare. It felt like the earth gave way right beneath her. Time stood still, and they were both speechless.

"What's is going on?" she said clenching her teeth. There was no need to ask because she heard the conversation. Still, he needed to explain.

Anderson looked down then looked away. He was finally able to make eye contact with her.

"Tiffany it's just some girl I met that's mad because nothing happened between the two of us. She acts crazy sometimes and I didn't want to make her upset. There are some fragile elements to her brain."

"You're leaving a lot of things out of the story. It's mighty funny that now she's crazy. Don't insult my intelligence. I know what I heard."

Anderson gently grabbed her by the shoulders. He could feel her shaking out of anger. Water welled up in her eyes, and a single tear fell down her cheek.

"Look, I met her years ago when I went into a Sprint store to get a phone. We started up a conversation and exchanged numbers. Yes, we went out a few times. She cooked me dinner, stuff like that. But once I made it clear that there could be nothing between us, she kinda lost it. So, Tiff, whatever you thought you heard was all in your head."

Maybe he was telling the truth. Maybe she should stop doubting him. Anderson has always been good to her and cared a lot about the feelings of others.

"Okay, Anderson. I believe you. I just thought I heard you..."

He put his finger up to her lips.

Whispering, he said, "Why in the world would I do anything to lose you? You're my future wife, and one day will be the mother of my child. You've been hurt so much in the past that your mind is playing tricks on you. Just let me love you. Now let's get out of here so we can forget all about this. I can give you that foot massage you always like."

Tiffany smiled and took his hand. She was so lucky to have him. So many other women long for a relationship with a good, successful man. There was no way she would give this up. Even if the woman on the other end liked him, Anderson was with her.

"Some women are so desperate," she thought.

A sense of calm came over her as they walked down the hall into the restaurant to leave.

Anderson opened the door for her as they headed outside. The cool air felt so good as it brushed against her face.

The valet brought his Jaguar around front.

"You still hungry Tiff? I'm sorry our date night was ruined, but we can still grab a bite to eat and take it to my house."

Her appetite had left her after the emotional moment at the restaurant.

"Nah, I'm good."

"You sure?"

"Yea, I just want to relax. Can we go to your place?"

~~~~~~

Anderson keyed in the code to the gate of his house. He drove up the winding driveway and parked in the garage.

Tiffany always loved it his home. It was regal, elegant, and classy. With its five bedrooms, it seemed almost too big for Anderson, but he was always one to do it big.

The front door was made of glass, lined with bronze, and stood about ten feet tall. As he unlocked the door, she envisioned the day when it will be her home as well.

Anderson walked straight into the kitchen rubbing his stomach.

"Man, that Five Guys fast food is gonna make me gain some weight."

"Serves you right Anderson. Did you need three burgers?" she asked.

"Haha. I'm gonna go hit the shower and when I come back out, we can binge watch some more of Luke Cage."

Anderson kissed her and walked towards the bathroom.

"Okay. I'd love that. We agree on a show, so I wouldn't pass that up. Hurry up."

Turning on the tv, she scrolled down the guide to see what was on. There was nothing that caught her attention.

"Gosh there is nothing on," she whispered.

She switched the tv mode and turned around to grab the Apple TV remote. There it was, his phone.

Anderson had no idea that she knew his password. Being one of those women who snoop didn't make her proud of herself.

She remembered telling one of her friends, "Girl, if you have to go through his phone, there's no trust. Plus, it wouldn't make me feel good. It's kinda childish."

Now, the tables have turned. She's the woman picking up the phone to try to confirm what she was feeling. There was no turning back now. The battle between her heart and mind had to end. This was it, her chance to find out what he was hiding from her. What she read took her breath away.

"Man that was the best shower in the world, I feel so relaxed," Anderson said while walking into his bedroom. He stopped dead in his tracks. Tiffany was standing there holding his phone.

All of a sudden, she threw the phone at him in a fit of rage. He quickly dodged out of the way, looking at her with shock in his face.

"I read all of the texts. I'm gonna marry you? I can't wait until you're the mother of my child? I enjoyed the Bahamas last year? You lied to me Anderson!" she screamed.

"You lied to me and you made a fool out of me. You said these same things to me. This isn't just some girl you know. According to these text messages, she's the love of your life."

The room was quiet and cold. It used to feel so warm and welcoming, but now it felt like a prison cell. She sat down on the side of the bed, putting her head in her hands, rocking back and forth.

"Not again. Oh my God. Oh my God."

Anderson walked up to her and said, "What are you talking about? Why are you acting like that?"

She looked up at him and he looked like a different person. He became cold just like the room standing there in his black robe.

"Look, I'm going back into the living room. When you calm down you can join me."

This was a dream. He saw her tears and her pain but did nothing to make them go away this time. Not once did he put his arms around her. There was no explanation or begging her for forgiveness.

"No. We're gonna talk about it right now. I'm tired of this Anderson. Tired of feeling this pain in my gut telling me that something isn't right. I'm tired of the burden of feeling like I have to be better or look better so that you won't want whoever that is on the phone."

He walked towards the door and turned around.

"Okay Tiff, you want the truth? I'm just tired and over this. You're not the only one pretending."

There it was, that stuffy feeling in her brain. There is no way this was real. Suddenly, tears she didn't know existed fell from her eyes.

He threw up his hands.

"See? That's what I'm tired of!" he yelled.

A look of surprise was on her face.

"You're too sensitive and insecure Tiffany. I can't keep explaining things to you. As a matter-of-fact, this is the time for me to come clean. Yes, I am seeing her. You want to know why? Because she makes me happy. She understands me, knows what I want. You try to, and your efforts are appreciated. But this is just the last straw."

Looking up at him with pain in her eyes didn't matter.

"So, we're over, just like that?

Her anger turned to sadness and she held back tears.

"Yes, we are," Anderson replied. I don't mean to hurt you, but I can't live a lie or hide my true feelings."

"How long have you been seeing her Anderson?" she asked.

"Don't worry about that Tiffany."

The apology and statement about not wanting to hurt her brought out a sense of rage. How did the love of her life talk to her like this? Where did her sweet Anderson go?

Tiffany's stomach was tied in knots. She was barely able to breathe. Two years of a relationship and planning to get married in a year turned into nothing.

"What am I supposed to tell everyone, Anderson?"

She looked down at her ring finger and thought about the fact that she and her sisters were looking at bridesmaid dresses just a week ago. Venues were about to be booked and registries had been created.

"What about our wedding, our life we promised each other?"

Her voice shook.

Anderson shrugged his shoulders. "I don't know. Tell them whatever you want to tell them. This breakup is on you. You're the one that is so weak that you can't keep a man. Too messed up is what I think."

She should've never told him about her past relationships. Now, he's using the stories like darts to bring her down.

"I could tell them you're a cheat."

He casually glanced her way. He didn't care, he looked happy.

"They're your family and friends. You're a smart woman. I'm sure you will find the words."

All Tiffany could think about was how she and her mother bonded so much during the wedding planning. Her law practice made it hard to hang out with her lately, so it meant the world to her.

They went to lunch just a few days ago and discussed this special time in her life.

"Baby, I'm so happy for you. I know you waited for so long for this moment. Now it's here just for you."

"I know mommy. I've always looked at love from the outside in, and now I have it."

"I can't wait for my grandkids. Oh, I'm gonna spoil them so much."

"Kids? Okay mommy, let's slow don't just a bit."

A feeling of embarrassment fell over her. This can't be true, she thought.

Getting up from the bed, she walked down the winding staircase into the living room.

"Bye Anderson."

He glanced her way and didn't say a word. She grabbed her purse and keys and headed out the door.

Yes, she would have a meltdown later, just not in front of him. The numbness in her spirit helped her to walk out with at least an ounce of dignity. As she walked out towards her car, a million thoughts crossed her mind.

He had complete control over her. It didn't happen when they first started seeing each other but over time. He used her pain from previous relationships against her, making her feel as if she needed him.

The tragedy in the situation was that she told herself that she couldn't live without him. He could talk to or treat her any way he wanted.

Picking up her phone, she started to call home, but then put the phone down. She needed to be consoled, but how could she explain this to her mother and father?

"How can I explain to her friends and co-workers that there won't be a wedding?" she thought.

Friends and family always came to her for encouragement and

advice and for the first time in her life, she didn't know what to do.

"It'll be okay, just take it a day at a time. If he can't see the value in you, you don't need him."

This is what she would say to her friends when they were going through dysfunctional relationships.

It was rough out there, and she was past the immaturity of some of the men she met. Anderson was her gold, and she held onto him for dear life.

She just sat in the car, looking out of the window. Her anger made her want to punch through the glass or tear the rearview mirror from the windshield. It wouldn't do any good though, she would only be hurting herself.

It started to rain, and Tiffany thought that it was right on time. It was raining in her heart, in her whole life.

"Good Love" by Anita Baker was playing. There was no way she was going to listen to it. As she reached out to turn it off, she heard a line that pierced her heart.

"I don't quite understand why loving me is so hard."

~~~~~~

2 EQUILIBRIUM

Tiffany opened her eyes and stared at the ceiling fan going in circles. Being awake was scarier than the nightmare she had from the situation with Anderson.

"God, I'm so scared," she whispered.

All of a sudden, she felt sick to her stomach and ran to the bathroom. The stress of the situation caused her to throw up. Her body couldn't take it anymore.

She crawled back into her bedroom and reached for her phone.

"Hello? Mommy?"

"Tiff? Everything ok?"

"Oh, yea. Sorry to call so early."

"Is everything ok baby?"

"Oh yea, I was just wondering if you'd checked on the venue for the reception yet."

She couldn't tell her why she called. The strong pride she carried held back the truth. There wouldn't be a wedding and she just needed her mother."

"I'm going today. Mr. Junai said to meet him at ten to confirm the date and give him a headcount. He said it's a good thing to do it in advance, so we're in a good position. I'll be sure to call you once I finish meeting with him."

"Okay mom, thanks. I love you and I'll call you later. Bye."

Taking a deep breath, she decided to go to work as staying home the day before proved to be more difficult than working.

Sadly enough, she caught a glimpse of the garment bag in the back of her closet holding her wedding gown.

"Girl, you should let your mother keep it at her house. You don't want it to get messed up in this horror of a closet," her friend Angie joked when she brought it home.

"Oh no. This will have a special place in my closet. Yes, it's six months away, but I don't want it out of my sight."

Anderson told her that she should have waited when she told him that she bought it. He wanted her to be sure that's what she wanted. Now she realized that he wanted to be sure if he wanted her.

~~~~~~

Before entering the building, Tiffany took a deep breath, forced a smile, and walked in.

"Good Morning Ms. Leroux."

Brandon was such a sweet man. He has worked for security for her firm for ten years now.

"Brandon. Hey." With all of her might, she was able to work up a smile. Still, she felt as if Brandon could see right through her. It's always in a person's eyes. Her grandmother used to tell her that, and it was true.

After opening the door and walking towards her office, she felt a sigh of relief that Ana wasn't at her desk at that moment. Small talk was the last thing she wanted to do.

Walking quickly past Ana's desk, she unlocked her office door and walked in.

Everything felt weird to her, almost like the conversation with Anderson never happened. She didn't feel anything now and realized that her mind was in shock. There was a knock at her door.

"Miss Leroux, I apologize for being late. The traffic was horrible...there was an accident on the freeway. I'm lucky I got here when I did," Anna said in her chipper voice.

"No problem Ana. Glad you made it here safely. Can you hold my calls until ten?"

Tiffany's voice sounded weak and exhausted. Maybe Ana didn't notice.

18

"Okay, well I'm going to get some coffee started. I'll go get your agenda for the day as well. Be right back."

As she walked away, it was evident to Tiffany that Ana stayed out all night. Her hair was a mess and she looked like she belonged in a club.

Glancing at the pictures on her desk, she reminisced about the trip to Italy she took with Anderson. She couldn't hold back her tears anymore

"What am I supposed to do without you, Anderson?" she whispered.

Tiffany covered her mouth and muffled the biggest cry ever. If they were having serious problems, it would have made more sense.

How long had this affair gone on? Did she know her? What was it that she had that made Anderson leave after so many years? All she could think about was how she just knew that her heartbreaks were over once she connected with Anderson.

"Oh my God, my head."

Frantically grabbing her purse and turning it upside down, a prescription bottle fell out. She hated taking pills for her anxiety but realized it was just her cross to bear. As she opened the bottle, her hands started to shake and the bottle fell on the floor, spilling pills everywhere.

"Oh no. What in the world?" she said as she got down on her hands and knees, scooping them back into the bottle.

Still, on the floor, she reached for the bottle of water on her desk and took a pill. All she could do at that moment was bring her knees up to her chest and sit against the wall. Super Tiffany didn't exist anymore.

After a few minutes, her heart stopped racing and her headache subsided just a bit.

Tiffany got up and walked over to the picture of her and Anderson across the room. She stared at the way they smiled and could see the joy in her face. All of her co-workers would comment about how they made such a wonderful couple.

"We were so happy then," she thought.

Suddenly, she threw the gold picture frame against the wall. What would her life look like now? Anderson meant the world to her and they went through good and tough times together. He was her rock, and she never thought she'd be facing the fact that he would no longer be in her life.

Just a text from him to say "I love you. Have a good day" helped her to deal with the most stressful of days. Reaching for a tissue, she realized there were none left.

Her phone rang. Ana was supposed to hold her calls but didn't listen.

"Hello, Ms. Leroux speaking."

"Hello, Miss Leroux, My name is Payton Baptiste and I was wondering if I could have a moment to speak with you."

The voice she heard on the other end was soothing and she felt like she'd heard it before.

"Did I catch you at an inconvenient time?"

"No. How can I help you?"

He spoke slowly, almost as if his life hung on every word.

"I would like to make an appointment to discuss a serious personal matter," he said.

Tiffany could hear the urgency in his voice.

"My nephew is in deep trouble and my friend referred me to you, said you're the best in the area. He told me that you defended his sister when she'd killed her father in self-defense. Sarah Wilson, I think?"

Payton was referring to her first case with Sarah.

"Windson. It was Sarah Windson. It was a difficult case. Yes, I can meet with you. I'm going to transfer you back to my assistant Ana to schedule our meeting."

"Sure, thing Miss Leroux. Thank you and I hope to meet with you soon."

Tiffany stood up and gazed out of her office window. All of a sudden, her door flung open.

"Miss Leroux I was wondering if you could…" Ana looked at Tiffany in shock. She knew something was wrong.

"Are you ok?" Ana asked.

Tiffany lowered her head to try to conceal how swollen her eyes had become from crying. She wished Ana would learn how to knock.

"Yes, I am. I'm not." Tiffany paused for a moment. "Cancel my 1:00 today. I'm not feeling well."

"Okay, Miss Leroux. Please let me know if you need anything."

"I sure will Ana, thanks.

3 AFTERMATH

Tiffany unlocked her door and walked into the living room. She immediately turned on the tv because the silence was too loud for her. Sitting on her brown plush sofa, she laid her head down on a throw pillow.

The memories of her breakup with Michael long ago came back to her mind. Sitting there, on that same couch, she wondered why she was always feeling pain. The scariest moment happened one lonely night when she was in a daze from drinking.

"Hello, dad?"

"Hey, Tiff. I thought you'd be in bed right now. Is everything ok?" he asked.

At that time, she could barely speak, but she needed help.

"I just can't take it any more daddy. Michael...," she said in a low voice.

Her father sighed. "Tiffany, don't talk like that. Did you do anything to hurt yourself again? You're mother and I can't stand to see you in that hospital again."

Barely holding the phone, she looked down and ran her fingers across the scars on both wrists.

"Tiffany!"

"Yes dad, I'm here."

"I'm on my way right now."

"Daddy there's no need to drive so far. I'm ok."

He paused.

"Look, I'm calling Angie right now. You stay on this phone. You hear me?"

"Ok, daddy."

And with that, she curled up in her bed while her father talked to her and quoted scripture. Once Angie arrived at her house and got on the phone with her father, he told her that he would be arriving the next day.

After that night she promised that she would never allow herself to get to that place again. Now she must tell him about Anderson and pray that he won't worry.

Thirsty, she headed for the kitchen to get a drink of water, but she found herself on her knees. Looking up to heaven, praying for understanding. All she could do was sit there and cry.

"Tiffany, even if you can't speak, God hears your cry."

Grandma's words spoke to her spirit.

She pulled herself up and headed to the bedroom. There was the black satin pillow he slept on only a few days ago. He laughed when she bought it for him. Explaining the benefits of sleeping on a silk pillow made him agree to use it. She smiled as she remembered the conversation.

"Look silly. It's good for your hair and your skin. It won't dry them out."

She gave him a friendly shove and he took the pillowcase, rubbing the fabric.

"Okay, Tiff. I'll try it. Only because I want to stay fly!"

The smell of his cologne was still on his pillow. A smile ran over her face and she felt a sense of warmth.

Still squeezing her pillow, her hopes, and dreams, she drifted off to sleep.

~~~~~~

The sound of the phone jolted her awake.

"Hello?"

"Hey, baby girl!"

Tiffany laughed to herself as her dad always sounded so cheerful. No matter how old she was, she was always his baby.

"Hey, daddy!"

Her attempt to put some life in her voice was harder than she thought.

"What's wrong?" her dad asked.

"Nothing daddy, just tired. I've been working on this case and it is wearing me out."

"Now I know you better than you think." He said with a laugh. She couldn't hold it in anymore. Her dad was always there each time her heart was broken. This happened so many times that she swore her dad picked up the energy of her broken heart.

"Anderson said that he just doesn't want to be with me anymore. Why? What about our wedding?"

Her father paused.

"I'm sorry, I know it hurts, but did you need him before and will you need him in the future?"

"Daddy this time is different. Anderson was my soulmate. He was my reason for breathing."

"Tiffany, what I want you to understand is that a wedding is a wonderful event, but at the end of the day, it's about who you're marrying. Anyone can put on a wedding, but it's your heart that matters. You hear me?"

"Yea. I don't even know how to tell mom. She was so happy."

"Do you need me to come up there? I don't want you struggling like you did the last time with Michael. Remember, you promised that you won't let a man take your joy."

"I'll take it in stride daddy. Is mom there?"

"Yes, hold on one moment."

Tiffany's heart sank. She hated to tell her mother that all of their hard work and planning was for nothing.

"Hey, sweetie. How are you? Your dad looks worried."

"There won't be a wedding. Anderson was cheating, he broke up with me. I'm so sorry."

"Now wait one minute. You'd better no apologize. He was the one that did wrong. God intervened and showed you that before you exchanged vows. It hurts, but you will look back and understand."

Her words were comforting, but she still felt that her mother was disappointed.

"I'll try to remember that mom. I'll be okay. I hate to cut the conversation short, but I'm gonna get some rest. I'll be sure to call you later," Tiffany said.

"Okay. Please remember what I said."

"I will love you."

She realized that she hadn't eaten all day and walked into the kitchen.

"Leftovers, leftovers, leftovers."

As she reached for the spaghetti, she saw the bottle of wine she shared with Anderson a few days ago.

"I don't like the taste of alcohol Anderson."

"Woman just try it. It has a different, sweet taste to it."

Tiffany frowned and said, "Okay. I guess it won't hurt."

"So? What do you think?"

"I hate to say that you're right Anderson, but you're right. I love it."

~~~~~~~~~~~~~~~~~~~~~~~~~~~~~~~~~~

4 INTRODUCTION

It was a beautiful Sunday morning as the sun was shining through the blinds. Sundays were always such a bright day for her. A day to feed her spirit, thank God for bringing her through another week and look forward to another one.

Today, there was a heaviness in her spirit. Picking up her phone, she decided to call her best friend Angie.

"Hey, Angie. You going to church today?"

"Yea Tiff. Are you?"

"I guess. I'm running late, so if you get there before me, just text me to let me know where you're sitting."

"Sure thing. I'll see you in a little bit."

Angela had been her friend for 18 years. They've been through so much together over the years. Leaning on each other during breakups, school, and even health problems.

Angela didn't know about the breakup. Tiffany decided to wait because she couldn't stand an "I told you so" speech. Angela warned her all along about Anderson, that he wasn't trustworthy.

~~~~~~

"Hey girl!" Angela yelled as she stepped out of the car. Tiffany tried to put on her best face and smiled.

"Hey! How's it going?"

"It's been okay Tiff. Crazy week, but I'm here." Angela said while walking fast and breathing heavily. Tiffany prayed that the swelling in her eyes didn't show. Angela always notices everything.

"Good morning," the usher said as he opened the door for both of them.

As they walked into the main sanctuary, the praise team

was singing.

"Grateful, grateful, grateful, grateful. Gratefulness," the choir sang as the sound reverberated off the brown wooden walls.

Tiffany clapped her hands and swayed from side to side, but still felt empty, angry, and depressed. Was God punishing her? Did He even care about her anymore? Still, she pressed on.

The lyrics of the songs filled her mind, yet she made a list of why she lost yet another relationship. Maybe it was because she and Anderson didn't wait until marriage to be intimate. Maybe she put him first above all else, even before God.

"Lord I need you," she whispered.

Wearing a long dark blue robe, the Pastor went up to the pulpit and looked at the congregation.

"Oh give him thanks, saints! He's been mighty good to you. Where would we be without his love."

The church erupted with hallelujahs, amens, and hands lifted to the sky. People were smiling, crying, and rejoicing, everyone but her. The praise break ended, but Tiffany wasn't a part of it.

"Today we will be reading from Psalm 23," Pastor Coreil said.

She opened her Bible to the chapter and verse projected on the screen. It had always been her favorite chapter.

"You see, verse four says, "Yea, though I walk through the valley of the shadow of death.""

"Yes it does," said a member of the congregation.

He continued and stated, "It says walkthrough. Not standstill, but walk. Through means, you will get to the other side. That other side is victory. A valley doesn't stay down flat, it goes back up."

These words spoke to her spirit letting her know that God was there. She couldn't just go off of what she felt, it had to be what was the truth.

"So I encourage you, saints, walk down the valley, let God guide you through that shadow. When you come out of whatever you're going through, you will see that there is absolutely nothing too hard for God."

As he continued his message, Tiffany felt lighter within her spirit. She was so focused on how disappointed God was with her that she forgot to receive His love and guidance.

"He's right here. You don't have to find him, he's right here in your heart, mind, and your world. This isn't the end for you."

She stood up along with the other saints and lowered her head.

"I'm gonna be okay. I'm gonna be okay," she whispered.

It didn't matter who was looking at her, it wasn't about them, it was about God. He did care about her and her aching heart.

Music started to softly play, "Amazing Grace" as the Pastor wrapped up his sermon.

Tiffany closed her eyes and took in every word of the song.

"Everyone have a blessed week and remember...God first, last, and always."

As the church emptied, people stood around talking and hugging in the lobby.

"You wanna go to lunch Tiff?"

"Oh girl, my cramps are killing me so I'm gonna head home and curl up into a ball."

She felt so bad about lying to Angela, but she wouldn't be good company.

"Ok. Call me later," Angela said.

"You know I will, girl."

After they hugged and parted ways, Tiffany stopped and rummaged through her purse looking for the car keys when someone bumped into her.

"Oh, I'm so sorry ma'am."

"It's okay, I wasn't looking where I was going. Excuse me."

They intensely locked eyes and just stood there.

"Well, have a good day," she said while walking away.

"You too."

"Miss Leroux, Mr. Baptiste is here to see you."

Tiffany forgot that she had a 9:00 appointment. Ana was late and usually hands her the agenda for the day. Sure, she received her appointments and agenda by email or on the calendar on her iPhone, but she always preferred to have it printed out.

"Ok, thank you, I'll be right out."

She walked towards Anna's desk and saw a man with beautiful mahogany brown skin and an athletic build wearing a black two-piece suit. He was the man she saw in the church lobby.

"Oh my God! It's him. Please don't let him remember me." she whispered to herself.

She smiled and reached out to shake his hand.

"Mr. Baptiste, glad you could be here. Please, come into my office."

He walked into her office and before sitting down, he began looking around at her pictures. Some of them were of her family, but most were of her and Anderson at their various vacation spots.

"Wow, you have a beautiful family. You travel a lot, huh?"

"Yes, I do."

"I see. Is this your man? Cute couple," he said picking up the picture.

"Are you two married?"

Tiffany shot him a look. He was intrusive and she began to get irritated. This meeting wasn't about her personal life.

He took his gaze from the pictures and turned his attention towards her.

"First off Ms. Leroux, I would like to thank you for taking the time to meet with me."

His eyes were deep and intense, and it was hard for her to maintain eye contact. His gaze intrigued and intimidated her, yet she liked the feeling.

"Of course, Mr. Baptiste. I'm happy to be of help," Tiffany replied while trying to maintain her composure.

"So, Mr. Baptiste, you mentioned that you had a family member who's in trouble?" Tiffany asked.

"Yes, deep trouble. I don't know if he's going to make it through this situation. Like I said before, I'm coming to you because I heard you're the best. Dedicated and concerned, not just out for money."

"Thanks. I appreciate that. We do the best we can here, everyone deserves good representation and justice."

"Well, my nephew is in big trouble. He's been wrongly accused of armed robbery, and there is no way he did it."

Tiffany could hear the concern in his voice and that he deeply cared for his nephew.

"Okay, tell me more. Does he have an alibi?" she asked.

"More importantly, why didn't he come to this meeting?"

He let out a nervous laugh.

"Well, you know how these young people are. They don't take anything seriously. I told him I was going to come and talk to you today, so he decided to stay home."

"I understand that Mr. Baptiste, but he should be here to give me the information you may not have. Getting third-hand information won't be precise enough."

"Okay, what should we cancel the meeting for today.?

"No, I can get a little bit of information from you but he must be at the next meeting. It's required, especially in the beginning. My team and I need to come with a strong game plan from the start, not halfway through," she replied.

She pulled out her notepad.

"So, since they arrested him, they have probable cause," Tiffany said while biting her lip.

"That's not good."

"Not Mr. Baptiste."

"Well, they say they have my nephew on surveillance camera. He was with me all that night. It's almost as if they won't let up because they want it to be him. I don't know if the DA wants to add a win under his belt or what." Payton said.

Tiffany paused.

"Do you have any other ways to show that he was with you? Did you go bowling or to a store, somewhere where you could be shown on camera? For example, if you went to Wal-Mart, you would be shown walking in or out of the store. Or, do you have a friend or family member that can help to provide a more solid alibi?" she asked.

"Well, we did go out to eat and then, went to my house where we hung out for the rest of the night."

"Mr. Baptiste, the reason why these details are important is because District Attorney Linwood is tough. He had won cases where many thought the defendant would win. And the evidence he presents, well, we never see it coming."

"I understand."

"Do you remember the case about Sara Windson?"

Payton shook his head and leaned forward in his seat.

"Well her mother was beating her mother, almost to death. So she ended up defending her mother, hurting him in the process. DA Linwood ruined her character so badly in court that she ended up looking like a monster. Her father looked like the injured victim. Do you see what we're up against?"

"I figured that. He is out for blood, huh?"

"Always. His team is notorious for presenting evidence that no one would expect to see. We have to have something stronger than the fact that you said he was with you," Tiffany stated.

"Wow. I don't have any other proof. That's why I'm concerned." Payton said.

"We were hanging out at my house playing games on my X Box. The fact that they are blaming him is ridiculous. The robber had on a hoodie and his face was barely visible."

"Mr. Baptiste, I understand but..."

"Please, Miss Leroux. I didn't mean to interrupt you, but I can't have my nephew be another black man caught up in the prison system. He's only 17 and has a whole life to live. There's a chance that it could be taken away." Payton said.

Tiffany took a deep breath.

"This is going to be a challenge, but I'll take this case and my team and I will do the very best we can. We will need to set up a meeting with you and your nephew to talk about this in-depth. I'll need to know all of the details of his day, who he was with earlier, etc."

Payton stood up and said, "Thank you, Miss Leroux. He will be at the next meeting."

He reached out and shook her hand again. His hand was soft, yet strong. A surge of energy went through her body. She quickly let go of his hand and cleared her throat.

"You're most certainly welcome Mr. Baptiste, I look forward to meeting with you and your nephew soon."

"Likewise. Have a great rest of your day," he said as he got up to leave.

She let out a sigh of relief as he didn't remember she was the woman who was staring at him during their encounter at church.

He suddenly stopped at the door and turned around.

"Didn't I see you at church the other day?"

He winked, grinned, and walked out of her office.

5 SENTIMENTAL

Tiffany was so glad to be home after her workout. The mere thought of working out exhausted her, so she was proud of herself for going. Her last visit to her psychiatrist wasn't exactly truthful.

"Are you working out Miss Leroux?" her doctor asked.

"Yep."

"Three days a week?"

"Yes, ma'am. Cardio and weights."

"Good. Keep it up. Exercise makes a difference mentally and physically."

She lied through the whole session. The only thing she wanted to do after work was go to sleep.

After taking a much-needed shower, she put on her favorite pink pair of pajamas and went into her bedroom.

Her bed was inviting, so she laid down under the covers and pulled the comforter up to her head and drifted off to sleep. It was two hours later when she woke up, almost time to go to sleep.

Her white Beats headphone rested on her nightstand. Tiffany connected it to her phone and turned up the music as loud as she could without damaging her hearing.

Knowing it was a bad idea, she played "Far Away" by Marcia Ambrosus. It always touched her soul as the lyrics described how a person feels when they miss someone.

"And every minute you're gone, I'm missing you so."

The words matched her life and her thoughts.

She rolled over and rubbed the side of the bed where Anderson used to sleep. They laughed about who owned what side of the bed, and it made her heartache that she would no longer have that conversation. She owned the whole cold, lonely bed.

"He'll call. He'll be here. He just needed some time and he'll realize that he made a mistake." Tiffany thought to herself.

Although she was hurt to the core, she decided that she would take him back. Nobody's perfect and they could work it out because love conquers all.

Her mind became jumbled as she refused to believe how her life was. Suddenly, she felt it. The trembling, nausea, and the feeling as if she was having a heart attack. It was a panic attack.

Tiffany ran into the living room and laid down on the couch. She grabbed a pillow and held onto it for dear life. Her attacks made her feel as if she was outside of her body like she was floating, so she learned to hold onto something to keep her from feeling that way.

"Just breathe. I'm not going to die. I'll be okay," she whispered to herself. The sweat-soaked the inside of her robe as she closed her eyes tightly.

Tiffany's panic attacks started when she was a child. Whenever she experienced any type of emotional stress, it affected her mentally and physically. It felt like death was staring her right in her eyes.

She began to practice the breathing exercises her therapist taught her a few months ago.

"Miss Leroux, I want you to do this when you are going through a panic attack. Breathe in, hold for four seconds, breathe out, hold for four seconds, then breathe normally."

"But Dr. Morris, I feel like I'm gonna die. My chest feels like it's going to explode. Will it help? What if I'm driving when it happens?"

"Yes the exercise will help, but you have to realize that it's just your body reacting to stress. You won't die. It's more mental than anything else."

Tiffany repeated this process four times, and her racing heart began to slow down. She felt a sense of calm fall over her.

There was no one to hold her, to tell her that everything will be okay. Once again, she was there to be the so-called independent black woman left to deal with this alone.

6 GLOOMY FRIDAY

It was finally the end of another week, and Tiffany was anxious to leave the firm.

Since her breakup with Anderson, she welcomed the weekend. Everyone got on her nerves, even the cashier at Starbucks. Patience was not one of her virtues. Still, she needed to get out of the house for the weekend.

"Bye Ana. Have a good weekend."

"You too Ms. Leroux. Got plans with my man tonight."

"Well, both of you have a great weekend then."

"Will do."

As she drove away from the parking lot, she decided to call Angie.

"Hey, Angie. It's your girl."

"Happy Friday. What's going on?"

"Let's do lunch," Tiffany suggested.

"I thought you moved away homie," Angie said.

Tiffany always loved how Angie found ways to incorporate what she called "thug talk" into her conversations.

"Great Angie. I gotta run a few errands after work, so how's 4:00 at Brennan's? I could use a banana foster right now."

"Cool deal," Angie said.

"See you in a bit."

~~~~~~

"Hey lover, hey lover, this is more than a crush." Boyz to Men belted out as she stepped out of the shower.

She dried herself off in the mirror and examined her body. Was she shapely enough? Did Anderson start to see wrinkles and wanted a younger woman?

The fifty-dollar night cream and thirty-five-dollar eye cream were a waste of money.

Would he have stuck around if she had plastic surgery and had the body of a celebrity? That's what men like right? Maybe she should've worked out more. Tiffany didn't blame him, it was something she did wrong.

Walking into her closet, she searched through her clothes. The little black dress would do. She quickly got dressed and, once again scolded herself for running late. Picking up her phone, she called Angie.

"Let me guess, you're gonna be a little late once again."

"I'm sorry. I'll be about 20 minutes late."

"Lord have mercy. My friend Tiffany," Angie said.

"You owe me a banana foster then."

"Gotcha Angie."

~~~~~~

Pulling up to Brennan's, Tiffany sat in her car. She always has an enjoyable time with Angie. It was time to let her know about the situation with Anderson. She felt a sense of dread in her stomach.

She quickly checked her makeup and hair in the rear-view mirror. All of a sudden, there was a loud horn.

Opening the door, Angie hopped out of her car.

"Hey, hey, hey, my late sister."

They hugged and walked towards the restaurant. When they walked in, they noticed that it was more crowded as usual.

They were greeted by the hostess who seemed overly happy. Tiffany noticed that she had on a ton of makeup.

"How many this afternoon ladies?"

"Table for two please."

"Okay. Follow me."

They were escorted to their table and sat down.

"Whew. I'm starving Angie."

"Me too. Whatcha gonna get?"

Tiffany picked up the menu and squinted. "

I'm not sure yet. Lemme see."

The waitress skipped up to the table. She seemed happier than the hostess, which didn't seem possible.

"May I start you two off with a drink?"

"Sprite."

"And I'll have a water with lemon please."

They discussed their hectic work week and other things that happened throughout the week. The waiter came back to take their orders, and Tiffany sat quietly, clearing her throat.

"Okay now. I've been noticing lately that something has been going on with you," Angie said with a frown.

"You gonna tell me?"

Tears welled up in Tiffany's eyes and she tried to maintain her composure. Crying in front of people made her feel weak, and she worked hard to display only strength.

Taking a deep breath, Tiffany said, "Anderson and I broke up. I looked through his phone and saw that he's been seeing some woman named Erica. Don't know how long he's been cheating on me."

"Girl, you gotta be kidding me. That low down..."

Tiffany lowered her head down and a tear fell down her cheek. Angie grabbed her hand.

"Sweetheart, I'm so sorry. I didn't mean to be harsh. I just knew that he wasn't good for you. Although you thought you were happy, I could see that there was never any joy in your face."

Suddenly, Angie's phone rang. She looked at it, turned it off, and put in in her purse.

"Girl, I'm so tired of these telemarketers calling me. I put myself on the Do Not Call list and they still call me. I'm sorry, you have my full attention now."

"It's okay, Angie."

"So where were you when you found out?"

"At his house. We'd went out to eat and went straight to his house afterward. When he was in the shower I grabbed his phone and looked through it."

"Wow, Tiff. You gotta be kidding me."

"I know. I felt so terrible looking through it. I'd never had to do that before, but I had this feeling and needed to know what was going on."

"So did he even try to explain or deny? I can't believe this."

"At first he acted like he didn't know what I was talking about. After I grilled him for a bit, he came clean. He said he was tired of me."

"Tired? Of what?" Angie said with a frown.

"He said he was tired of my insecurities. It was if breaking up with me was a breath of fresh air."

Tiffany gazed out of the window and whispered, "Just be there for me Angie. Please don't give me the "you shoulda known" speech."

She picked up the napkin from her nap and wiped her eyes, hoping that no one was looking at her.

"First off, I'm in no position to judge you. I'm just so sorry. You know that I'm here. Even if you need me to just sit with you, eat ice cream and talk about how sorry these men are."

They both let out a laugh. Tiffany loved how Angie could find the humor in challenging situations. This is what she needed right now.

"Oh my God. I'll be right back," Angie said while holding her stomach.

"What's wrong?"

"Nothing. Just not feeling well. I'll be back in a minute."

Angie was gone for about ten minutes, then returned to the table.

"So? You okay?"

"Girl, I'm so nauseous. I have something to tell you. I'm…

"Pregnant?"

"Yea. I found out last month. I haven't told anyone because people are so judgmental. I'm not married to James, you know?"

"Girl, this time I'm not in any position to judge you. I've had my scares in the past," Tiffany said.

"It was such a shock. I'm still in denial, but as you can see, I have to accept it. My body is showing me that."

"I'm gonna be a Godmother! I can't believe it. Finally some good news in the midst of all of this negativity in my life."

Angie took a deep breath.

"I just have to find a way to tell my parents."

Tiffany leaned forward.

"Angie, just tell them. I'm sure they will be so excited. Parents always love grandkids."

"I know. They just pictured me being married first. Heck, I envisioned the same thing."

Tiffany threw up her hands.

"Girl, between my breakup and your pregnancy, we have to lean on each other."

"Yes, we do. One day at a time."

"How about we go to see "Man Underground?""

"Angie, I don't know. I just want to go home and hibernate under my comforter."

"Come on. It'll keep our minds off of these serious issues for a while."

Tiffany rolled her eyes.

"Okay. Yea. You're right."

Going out would be beneficial for her. Her days have been cold and lonely, and she was blessed to have a friend who would be there for her. They paid the tab and left the restaurant.

~~~~~~

It was 9:00 pm when Tiffany arrived home She pulled up to her garage and sat in the car for what seemed like forever. There was a feeling of numbness in her heart as the music played "The Lady in My Life."

"And I will keep you warm through the shadows of the night."

It was too much for her to listen to at the moment. Michael Jackson meant every word.

Tiffany turned the radio was turned off and continued to sit in the car in silence.

Opening the car door, she stood outside and looked up at the twinkling stars.

"If you could go up to the moon, would you go?"

She asked Anderson as they sat on a bench at the park after spending the day together years ago.

Pausing for a minute he replied, "Yes, I would go. Can you imagine the amount of engineering it takes to make that happen?"

She laid her head on his shoulder.

"I'd go, but then I'd be afraid that I wouldn't be able to get back."

They sat there in silence looking up at the sky. The fullness of the moonlit up the sky with love.

Now, she looked up and felt a loneliness so deep that she could see it in the stars.

Somewhere up there the memories of her happiness still existed.

This was the same sky that she and Anderson walked and loved underneath.

No one could take that moment away from her. Sure, the relationship wasn't real because it was based on lies. However, they would always be real to her because she loved him from the depth of her soul.

"Time to go in," she whispered to herself.

Into the dark, into an empty apartment with only silence to greet her.

~~~~~~

It was 9:00 pm when Tiffany arrived home She pulled up to her garage and sat in the car for what seemed like forever. There was a feeling of numbness in her heart as the music played "The Lady in My Life."

"And I will keep you warm through the shadows of the night."

It was too much for her to listen to at the moment. Michael Jackson meant every word.

Tiffany turned the radio was turned off and continued to sit in the car in silence.

Opening the car door, she stood outside and looked up at the twinkling stars.

"If you could go up to the moon, would you go?"

She asked Anderson as they sat on a bench at the park after spending the day together years ago.

Pausing for a minute he replied, "Yes, I would go. Can you imagine the amount of engineering it takes to make that happen?"

She laid her head on his shoulder.

"I'd go, but then I'd be afraid that I wouldn't be able to get back."

They sat there in silence looking up at the sky. The fullness of the moonlit up the sky with love.

Now, she looked up and felt a loneliness so deep that she could see it in the stars.

Somewhere up there the memories of her happiness still existed. This was the same sky that she and Anderson walked and loved underneath.

No one could take that moment away from her. Sure, the

relationship wasn't real because it was based on lies. However, they would always be real to her because she loved him from the depth of her soul.

"Time to go in," she whispered to herself.

Into the dark, into an empty apartment with only silence to greet her.

7 MESMERIZED

"Didn't I just lay my head down on the pillow!" Tiffany yelled as the alarm sounded.

She quickly hit the snooze button and tossed the cell phone on the floor. It continued to go off. There were no more snooze opportunities left.

Tiffany eventually sat up at stared at the wall. Since the breakup with Anderson, she wasn't motivated to do her morning prayer. Still, she could hear in her mind what her mom always says, "Pray whether good or bad."

She got down on her knees, resting them on her blue plush mat. Nothing came out, she just kept kneeling there, thanking God.

After a few minutes, she slowly got off her knees and headed for the bathroom. It was quite chilly, so she checked the thermostat and turned on the heat.

Letting out a loud sigh, she opened her medicine cabinet. There it was, her daily dose of happiness. This process was getting old, she'd been taking it for over ten years now following the advice of her doctor. Her first visit ten years ago is stuck in her mind.

"Miss Leroux, your depression is both environmental and genetic. If you don't take any medicine, it will only get worse as you get older."

"But I've tried medicine in the past. The only thing that

happened were side effects that made it hard to work."

Her voice began to tremble.

"Blurred vision, rashes, blisters on my fingers. How am I supposed to practice law when I'm dealing with all of this."

Her doctor scooted up to her desk and took off her glasses.

"Look, you will have to take it for the rest of your life. I know that's not what you want to hear, but at least you have the resources to treat your depression."

And with that, she left with her prescription.

The medicine wasn't pointless though. It at least lessened some of her depression and helped her to get up out of bed.

This was part of her morning routine, but she wished for once to not have to take anything to function.

~~~~~~

After her usual greeting to Ana and receiving her agenda, Tiffany walked into her office and placed her briefcase down in her chair. She stood looking out of the window, closed her eyes, and took a deep breath.

The sun was shining, and she could feel the warmth on her face. She was feeling better day by day, although she had her moments. The road was long, but a little progress was better than none at all.

"Miss Leroux, Mr. Baptiste is on line 2."

Tiffany picked up her phone, "Hello?"

"Miss Leroux?"

Tiffany rolled her eyes wondering why it seemed as if he didn't know it was her. Then again, she was irritated with men these days, so she brushed it off.

Taking a deep breath, she replied, "Good morning Mr. Baptiste."

"How are you?"

"I'm doing well, hope you are. Did I catch you at an inconvenient time?" he asked.

Tiffany was sure he heard the bitterness in her voice. She didn't do a good job hiding it at all.

"Of course not. I've been looking forward to hearing from you to schedule a meeting with Brandon."

It was so nice to hear his voice, and Tiffany became confused.

What was it about him?

"Hello?" There was such a long pause that Payton had to make sure that she was still on the phone.

"Oh, ummm…I'm sorry. An associate came to my door. What was that?"

"Lunch, I asked you what you were doing for lunch," he said.

She was so consumed in her thoughts that she didn't even hear his question.

Tiffany squeezed the phone not knowing how to answer his request. Was she his attorney or being asked on a date?

"Well, I…Mr. Baptiste, I would like to keep our interactions on a professional level," she said.

"I haven't even met with Brandon yet. I agreed to take his case not to go to lunch." She said in a stern voice.

Payton chuckled on the phone.

"I'm not asking you to marry me, just to go out to lunch, on a professional level. I'm sure you could use some air. How about we meet at August's?" he asked.

Tiffany realized that the office was a bit stuffy and she could use a change of scenery. Going against her instinct, she agreed to meet him.

Although this was a professional meeting it felt great to anticipate the company of a man. She grabbed her purse and walked out of her office.

"I'm going out to lunch Ana. Make sure you take down messages for me."

"Sure thing Miss Leroux," Anna said, barely looking up from her Essence magazine.

"Professional, professional" she kept repeating to herself.

"Good Afternoon ma'am. How many?"

"Oh, I'm meeting someone here."

Looking around she spotted Payton sipping on a drink.

He stood up to greet her as she walked up to the table. His dark blue short-sleeved Polo shirt revealed his muscles, but Tiffany pretended not to notice them.

As she reached out for a handshake, he hugged her. Her body temperature rose.

She missed being held like that but quickly pulled away. This was highly inappropriate for someone who reached out to be his nephew's client.

Much to Tiffany's surprise, he pulled out her chair for her. chivalry wasn't dead after all.

"Thank you."

"No problem. My father taught me well."

He smiled and all Tiffany could think about were those dimples again.

"Have you been here before?" he asked.

"No. I've heard a lot about it. Do you suggest anything?"

"Hmmm, lemme see."

Payton rubbed his chin as they both studied the menu. As he looked down, Tiffany looked at how handsome he was. He looked up and she had just enough time to look away.

"You like shrimp?"

"Yes."

"Okay, then. I would try the grilled pompano. The lime and ginger have a unique taste, but I think you'll like it."

"Well shrimp pompano it is," she said.

He held out a hand as if to tell her to stop.

"You know you can relax a bit because I don't bite," he said with a laugh.

Tiffany let out a sigh and smiled, attempting to relax.

"Is that better?"

"See. That's what I'm talking about. You're an attorney, but you can still show those pearly whites."

"You look beautiful today. I love your dress, by the way, it fits you well."

Tiffany looked down and said, "Thank you."

"Don't be modest Miss Leroux. You have a nice figure."

"Well, I try to work out when I can. Also, you can call me Tiffany."

She started to feel more comfortable with him, so it didn't feel weird to have him call her by her first name.

"Okay Payton, now that we're here laughing and joking, I must be serious for a second. Why are we here?"

Payton cleared his throat.

"My nephew is my life. I became a father figure to him ever

since his abusive father left. Brandon tried to be the man of the house and I couldn't let him do that. He was too young and needed to focus on his education. He should be looking at what colleges he wants to go to. You know, things like that. Now, this."

Sadness fell over his face and he looked off into space as if he was in another world.

"He left Brandon and his mother high and dry. They had a beautiful home and almost lost it all, but I was able to hold them down until his mother found a job. They're okay financially, but no amount of money can buy a father."

"I agree Payton."

"I promised his mother that I would always be there, so I have to handle this situation."

"Mr. Baptiste. I understand that. I mean, he's family, so that makes sense. You want the best for him." Tiffany said to him.

Payton moved forward, and the faint scent of cologne hit her nose

He looked deep into her eyes.

"What I'm trying to say is that I don't want him to be just another black man in the prison system. Brandon always says that he wants to be an engineer like his uncle. I can't let him down," he said almost whispering.

"If he is found guilty of armed robbery, they will charge him as an adult. He's 17, legally they can do that to him."

Tiffany looked down and pushed the food around on her plate. "Mr. Baptiste, I mean, Payton, I will do all that I can to win this case. I can see how much you want the best for Brandon," she said.

"Please understand that I will use every resource to prevent him from being found guilty of this crime. Becoming a felon will negatively impact his life. He'll have a tough time finding a job, apartment, even voting," she told him.

Payton reached out and grabbed her hand. "Thank you," he said.

Tiffany expected to hear more from him, but she realized that his simple "thank you" and watering eyes said enough. It was evident that he was holding back. His vulnerability intrigued her.

She found herself still holding onto his hand and felt his pain and frustration. He was hurting for Brandon, and she was hurting for herself.

The energy of serenity covered her even though she just met him. He was looking to her for help, but she needed protection. It was just too soon. It was a moment... just a moment. Nothing more.

Payton added a warmness to her and made her feel as if she wasn't just a high paid attorney. She made a difference in people's lives and she would do all she could to show Prosecutor Linwood that Brandon didn't commit this crime. He has an uncle that cares about him and now she cares about his life too.

8 REVELATION

Tiffany waited for the rest of the associates to congregate into the conference room. She made partner after her father retired, but still felt a little intimidated when she had to call a meeting about a case.

"Okay everyone, we have a 17-year-old African-American male accused of armed robbery. His name is Brandon and his uncle, Clayton Baptiste, stated that is no way he committed the crime because they were together the whole evening."

She went into a small box and turned on the television. Placing the tape into the recorder she looked at the associates.

"Here's his photo and now we're going to look at the video footage."

The associates and paralegals leaned forward squinting their eyes while looking at the screen.

Sheila Pierce, one of the paralegals raised her hand as if she was in a classroom. Tiffany always found her annoying, always wanting to be the center of attention. She often used complex words straight from a law book to show that she was smarter than everyone else. Still, she had a right to ask questions as this was an important case.

Pursing her lips together she said, "No offense Miss Leroux, but he does look like Brandon. I don't think he will be found innocent."

The associates looked away from the tv and stared at Sheila.
I mean, everyone wants to play the race card these days. If he's guilty, then he's guilty," Sheila said rolling her eyes.

The room became dead silent.

Tiffany's heart began to race. Coming from a white woman, this statement added insult to injury.

Lee Hamilton, a first-year attorney, slammed his pen down on the desk.

"Are you serious? Black men are being shot for no reason. We have a case where one is falsely accused and can go to prison for no reason. I can't believe you right now. As a black man, I feel disgusted with you right now."

"Hey, you two. Let's calm down and remember that we show his innocence with proof, not emotions."

Looking Sheila in the eyes, Tiffany responded, "Mrs. Pierce, we can't jump to conclusions without looking at the facts."

Sheila lowered her head a bit and didn't even attempt to start another sentence. For the life of her, Tiffany couldn't understand why she even hired Sheila. The other associates often discussed how she often made racist remarks.

Lee turned towards Sheila.

"Mrs. Pierce, I apologize for raising my voice, but there is a life on the line right now. We know that we have a fight on our hands, but we can't go into this with a defeated attitude. Your racist attitude is way out of style."

The associates looked around, not quite sure what to do or say.

"Now that we're back on track we know that Prosecutor Linwood is a trickster and will go through all the evidence with a fine-tooth comb. Our job is to do the same. He doesn't play fair and is out for blood," Tiffany said.

Taking a deep breath, she looked everyone in their eyes.

"There are going to be some late nights. We can't let our client down."

The associates frowned and groaned.

"Since it's 6:00, we can all go home, but be ready to put on your A-game tomorrow. We need to start thinking about strategy, so I need you all to be focused. No slacking off."

The meeting was adjourned, and as everyone stood up to leave, Tiffany looked at their hands. They all had on a wedding rings except her.

"Good night Miss Leroux."

Richard was always polite. He was the hardest working associate and Tiffany just knew that one day he would make partner.

Smiling she replied, "Good night Richard. Be sure to tell Helen and the kids I said hello."

A wave of sadness fell over her.

They had husbands, wives, and children to go home to.

She had neither a husband or a child. Although she made partner, she felt like the smallest person in the room.

"You're a wonderful woman. Hardworking and changing lives," Payton said to her during lunch the day before.

She smiled and gathered her purse and briefcase.

A man she hardly even knew encouraged her for the day and didn't even know it.

~~~~~~

"Uggh. What in the world?" she said looking through her blinds.

Mr. Baker was using his extra loud lawn mower at 7 am on a Saturday. Trying to sleep in wasn't an option.

Walking into the kitchen, she decided to make breakfast. It was time to decide what to do for the day. She picked up her phone.

"Hey Jackson, it's Tiffany!" she tried to sound happy as well as bury the guilt she felt for not having seen her personal trainer for almost two months.

Jackson responded, "Tiffany, Tiffany. Hmmm, I don't know a Tiffany."

"I know I'm a stranger. I meant to return your calls a couple of weeks ago, but life has been so crazy."

"No worries! Glad you're alive man!" he said.

"We used to go hard, so let's get back to seeing some results because I know they're gone by now."

They both agreed to meet at 2:00. Tiffany was slowly starting to get her strength back. Day by day, she was beginning to get her focus back on her life again.

~~~~~~

Wiping the sweat off her face, Tiffany waved goodbye to Jackson. It was only 5:30, still too much time left in her day.

Deciding to return home, Tiffany sat down on her couch and turned on the tv, her usual routine. There had to be some activities going on.

She opened her laptop and scrolled through weekend activities in the area. Museum exhibits, no, water park, definitely not, food truck rodeo, not even on the radar.

Tiffany decided to find out what movies were playing. It was a wonderful place to go with her mindset right now. Entertainment, food, and it was dark. No one would be able to tell that she was alone.

"Top 5" was playing. She decided to buy her tickets online and quickly headed to the shower. The next showing was in 30 minutes.

Excitement, independence, life. These were her feelings as she took and shower and got dressed.

Feeling a sense of pride, she checked her hair and makeup and headed out the door. It was time to have a little fun, even if it was just for the duration of the movie.

~~~~~~

"Top 5" didn't disappoint. Tiffany laughed and it felt good. The other moviegoers were laughing and repeating lines as they walked out of the theatre.

The crisp night air filled her lungs as she walked towards through the lobby. It felt good to be in her Adidas, joggers, and favorite red fleece pullover. There was no pressure to look like a diva with sore feet and tight uncomfortable clothes.

"I shouldn't have had so much soda," she said to herself. It was too far of a drive to wait, so she headed towards the restrooms. As she turned the corner she saw Anderson waiting outside of the ladies' room and stopped dead in her tracks. He looked so handsome, and for a moment she forgot how much she hated him.

"Ummm. Hey," he said.

There was a look of shock on his face. It made sense as they hadn't seen each other in weeks.

"Hello."

"How's it going?" Anderson asked while looking around nervously. The fact that he asked her that question puzzled her. He knew exactly how she was doing.

"Good. Everything's good."

"Are you here alone, Tiff?"

"Well, I, umm. I met a friend here and he left already."
It was a lie, but she couldn't let him know that she was alone. The conversation made her uncomfortable.

"So, I gotta go. We're meeting for dinner as well," Tiffany said.

"Ok. Take care," Anderson replied.

Tiffany walked as fast as she could. Confusion, love, hate, and sadness were all wrapped into one. It was obvious that he wasn't alone. Knowing that he was already dating cut her heart like a knife.

"Where's my car?" Tiffany thought to herself.

She was so confused that she forgot where she parked. It was time to hit the panic button as it was time to go. There was no time to be wandering around in the parking lot. It would crush her to see Anderson and his date happily walking out together.

"There it is."

Tiffany quickly got into the car and froze. Her pain turned into rage, anger, and hate. She not only felt that way towards Anderson. The depth of the pain of every man who mistreated her seemed to take over her mind.

"It's me," she whispered. She would need to count beyond two hands how many guys she dated. Most of them went on to marry someone else.

Right now, they were enjoying being married, playing with their kids, enjoying vacations.

It was her. The common denominator in every one of her relationships.

This was her answer, her truth. She was the reason for her unhappiness.

~~~~~~

"I don't think you're being honest with me," Tiffany said to Brandon.

Crossing his arms and rolling his eyes, he responded, "Yes I am!"

Both Tiffany and Payton stopped and stared at the young man, surprised by his attitude. Brandon slumped down in his chair, hanging his head down.

Payton, sitting beside Brandon, leaned over towards him.

"Either you show some respect or we let you go to jail. Disrespect is not an option."

"Sorry."

Tiffany looked at them both. "Look, Brandon, I'm here to help you. Now that we've established the fact that you will respect me, we can continue building your defense."

"Brandon, you look people in the eye when they're talking to you. Pick your head up."

"Gosh, you're my uncle, not my dad."

"Payton, I need you to explain to your nephew how crucial his cooperation is. If he can't handle this from me, how will he handle it when he's crossed-examined by Prosecutor Linwood?"

"Who's that Mrs. Leroux? The boogeyman?"

Shooting Brandon another angry look, Payton shook his head.

"That's an understatement. He will tear you apart and have you serving 5 to 10 years."

"Nah bruh, not me."

Tiffany slammed her pen down on the desk.

"That's it. I'm done. Payton, this is ridiculous. In my years of practicing law, I've never felt so disrespected."

"Hold on lady, I never said I don't care. It's just that I ain't getting caught up when I didn't do it."

"Do you even care about the fact that Mr. Baptist wants the best for you? Huh? Do you!"

"Dag. Calm down lady, I mean Mrs. Leroux."

"People are just so inconsiderate these days. Walking over the people who've been there for them. I just don't understand it."

Payton looked back at Tiffany and their eyes met, almost locked onto one another.

"Ummm, Brandon, why don't you go grab some snacks from the vending machine. Here's some money."

They both waited until Brandon left the room.

"Tiffany, what's wrong?" he said in a soft voice.

She shuffled around some papers. "Nothing."

Payton leaned forward and said, "I beg to differ. You're up some days we meet, and there are times like today. You seem to be so closed up. So sad."

Her eyes began to water as he spoke.

He'd make comments to her before like this. It scared and amazed her at the same time. She took a deep breath and cleared her throat.

"I'm so sorry. I crossed the line by saying that."

Tiffany shot him an angry look.

"Yes, you did, Payton. I told you before that we need to remain professional."

There was no way she was going to tell him about the night at the movies. She enjoyed Payton's company and felt bad about being so cold to him. The little opening to her heart was closing again, even to him.

Brandon walked in with a Sprite and a bag of chips.

"Here you go uncle P. I bought you a bag of Doritos. Oops! I forgot to bring you a drink," Brandon said sarcastically.

Tiffany was so annoyed she wondered if she made a mistake by taking him on as a client.

"I think we can wrap up for the day you two. Ana will get with you on your way out to schedule you in for the next meeting."

Tiffany started to gather her things.

"Tiffany, can I please talk to you? Call you later?" Payton asked.

"I need to go. I have a lot to do."

Payton grabbed her briefcase and said, "Come out with me tonight."

Tiffany stopped in her tracks.

"Payton I…"

"Not a date, you can have an enjoyable time. Just as friends. Friends are still professional right?"

"Okay, but I'll drive my car."

"That's a bet! I'm gonna take Brandon back home and we can head out. Follow me."

Once they arrived at Brandon's house, he got out of Payton's car and walked towards Tiffany.

"Ma'am, I'm sorry for the way I acted. I guess pretending to be tough was easier than being scared."

"Brandon, I understand that you're scared. We'll take care of you, ok?"

"Okay."

He waved goodbye to both of them. Tiffany smiled. His apology warmed her heart.

Before they took off, Payton got out of his car and ran to Tiffany's window.

"Just checking on ya!"

"I'm okay. Just a bit tired," Tiffany replied

"Where are we going?"

"Just follow me."

~~~~~~

Payton, followed by Tiffany, pulled into the parking lot of Lois Armstrong Park. She always wanted to visit the park, but life was so busy.

When she turned off the car, he walked up to her door.

"Lemme open this for you."

He reached for her hand and guided her out of the car. That chivalry melted her heart every time.

"Thank you."

She looked around.

"This is nice. I've never been here. It's beautiful," she said while looking around.

They walked up to a bench and sat down. The breeze carried the scent of Payton's cologne. Tiffany took a deep breath to take it in.

Payton looked at her, "What's your biggest fear?

No one had ever asked her that before. She hung her head down deep in thought.

"Wow, that's random and unexpected. I'm facing them right now."

"You know, when I was a little boy, I had these stickers in my room that lit up when the lights turned off," he said.

"So even in the darkness, remember there will always be light."

Tiffany didn't respond.

"Hello? Are you there?" he asked.

"Mr. Baptist...I mean Payton, I'm not gonna go into detail, but I need to tell you this so that you won't take my negative moods personally. I'm dealing with a breakup."

"Oh wow, I didn't know..."

"Yea. I found out that he wasn't faithful. We were

supposed to get married and everything, that's it. I'm okay though."

Payton grabbed her hand.

"No, it's not Tiffany, and it's okay."

She was puzzled at his response and asked him what that meant.

"What I mean is, it's okay not to be okay. How do you feel?"

"What does that have to do with anything?"

"It means everything. How do you feel? Looking back, were there things you would've changed? I'm not in any way blaming you, what I'm trying to get you to see is what made him think that he could do that to you. Knowing this will give you more power in the future."

"I guess so."

"How could he let go of someone so beautiful. Not just outside, but inside."

"I don't know about that, but thank you."

"I would never make such a mistake. You don't even see how beautiful you are."

"Payton. You're saying what you're supposed to say."

"No. I mean the first time I saw you I knew you were special."

"Do you say that to all the ladies?" Tiffany asked with a slight smile.

"Ha, ha. No, I don't."

"Oh."

"I just want you to receive it and not deny it. I'll keep telling you that until you believe it. I give, you receive. Just say thank you."

"Thank you."

Payton glanced at his watch.

"Ah man, they close at 8. I don't want to leave. I'm enjoying talking with you aside from legal negative stuff."

"Yea, it has been nice Payton"

"I guess we can head on back to the cars now."

They stopped at Tiffany's car and stood beside the driver's door.

"Well Miss Leroux, I will be talking with you soon," Payton said.

"Come here Tiff."

Payton pulled her close to him and wrapped his arms around her. He moved his face closer to hers as if to kiss her. Instead, he whispered in her ear.

"Remember that light in the darkness, okay?"

As Payton turned and walked away, all Tiffany could do was stand there and stare.

~~~~~~

9 CONFUSION

"Go!" Tiffany screamed at the car in front of her.

She pulled into the parking lot of the law firm. A couple caught her eye.

It was Maria, one of the associates. Her husband Gary was dropping her off. He gave her a hug and a kiss. She looked up and spotted Tiffany.

"Hey Miss Leroux!" she said,

"Hello, Maria," Tiffany replied, waving through the window.

She gathered her things out of her car and headed into the building.

Expecting to see Ana, she once again saw Lawrence, a paralegal at her desk.

"Oh, Ana's in the restroom. Said she wasn't feeling well. I don't know." He shrugged.

Tiffany frowned and leaned forward to grab her agenda off her desk.

Tiffany opened her office door and put down her briefcase and purse. The message light was lit. It was Payton leaving a message with his soothing voice.

"Hey, Miss Leroux. It's Mr. Baptiste. I want to follow up with you regarding the meeting yesterday. Thank you for the hard work you've been putting in. I hope to have a conference with you soon."

Tiffany was puzzled, then started smiling. It was obvious that he wanted to leave a professional message at her place of work.

Although she enjoyed his company the other night, Tiffany didn't call him back immediately. She needed time to process her feelings and emotions.

Still, all she could think about were their tender moments from the night before. He was something special.

Tiffany turned on the jazz station on Pandora to start her day. The notes from Brandon's case lay on her desk. She picked up the phone to call Mr. Watson, a paralegal.

"Hey, Mr. Watson. Can you stop in my office for a minute?"

"Sure Miss Leroux."

"Thank you"

Mr. Watson stepped into her office,

"Good morning"

"Mr. Watson," Tiffany said with a smile.

"What do you have for me? How's the Brandon Baptiste case going?"

"Well, you'll be happy to know that we're making great progress."

"Awesome. Thank you all for your hard work."

"We talked to the right people, and found character witnesses for Brandon."

"Okay. So let's all meet at 2 tomorrow to go over the details."

~~~~~~

Tiffany missed her sister Lauren since she moved to New York City. She was happy that, after years of effort, her sister was finally able to be on the big screen.

"Here and Now," a romantic comedy, broke office records. Lauren was always inviting her to premiers and red-carpet events. Living vicariously through her sister allowed her to forget about her life for a while.

She thought for a minute and called her sister.

"I'm not speaking to you!" Lauren said with a laugh.

I haven't heard from you in weeks!"

Tiffany knew it was true. Since her break-up with Anderson, she hadn't been keeping in contact with Lauren. Maybe it was because her life was so messed up and Lauren's was exciting and progressive.

"I know, I'm sorry. There's been so much going on," Tiffany replied

"Enough about me Lauren. How's the new project going?"

She sighed and said, "It's going well but so many hoops to jump through. It's worth it in the end though because I've always wanted to direct. So, when am I gonna get to see my little sis again?"

Tiffany opened her mouth and then paused. How could she visit her sister with all this drama going on in her life? Then she remembered how she vowed to focus on herself.

"How about Saturday?" she asked.

"That'll work. The crew is taking a break, so that's perfect. I need some relaxation and fun."

"I could stay for about a week if that's okay."

"Tiff? You don't even have to ask."

"I know, but you're just so busy, so I wanted to check first."

She owed it to herself to take a trip. Especially after her vacation with Anderson fell through.

"I'll go ahead and look for some tickets."

"Ummm, excuse me? Your big sis has an assistant who will do that for me. I'm officially important."

"Okay, thanks a bunch."

"No problem. I'll be in touch with you soon. Love ya."

"Love you too, Lauren."

~~~~~~

"Really? New York?" Ana put her hands over her mouth.

"Yes, I know, it's unexpected." Tiffany laughed.

They discussed meetings, clients, and priority cases. Tiffany felt a tinge of guilt because she was taking a break. Brandon's life was depending on her, but what good would she be if she was burned out?

"So I will inform your clients that you will be gone all next week. If they have any questions, I'll forward them to an associate," Anna said.

"Sounds like a plan. Well, I'm gonna go to my office and start my workday."

"Alrighty. I'll make some coffee and bring it to you."

She picked up her phone to text Angie.

"What are you doing for lunch? Wanna grab a bite later?"

"If I can get away from these vultures at work I can do lunch. I swear they want me to sit at my desk and crunch numbers. They don't believe in taking breaks."

"Okay. Just let me know"

"Will do."

Ana walked up to her office door.

"Miss, Leroux?"

"Yes, Ana."

"Your conference with the team starts in 30 minutes."

"Thanks for reminding me. Make sure the other associates are there as well."

"Sure thing."

She opened walked over to her desk and picked up the phone, dialing Payton's phone number. Payton didn't know about her trip.

"Hello?"

Tiffany squeezed her eyes shut.

"Hi, Payton. I hope your day is going well. I umm, I'm calling to let you know that I will be out of town all next week. Carl Wavey is on the team and can help you should you have any questions or concerns."

"Awww man! Where to? Can I go?"

"No, sir!" she said with a laugh.

"I'm going to visit my sister Lauren. I just wanted to let you know, that's all."

Payton said that he understood and told her to be safe.

"It's a much-needed vacation for you. Life will be here waiting, take care of you."

"Thank you, Payton. I'll be in touch once I get back in town. I have a meeting starting at about 20 so I have to go. Have a great rest of your day, okay?"

"You too Tiffany. I hope the rest of your day goes well."

"I appreciate that. Same to you."

She leaned back in her chair and daydreamed for a minute. Looking at the time, she got up and walked out towards the conference room.

"Good morning everyone. It's time to get serious and discuss this so-called evidence Prosecutor Linwood has."

I have been informed that he has an eyewitness to the robbery. His uncle, Mr. Baptiste, stated that Brandon was with him the night of the robbery."

She looked around the room as she spoke.

"Our goal is to show that the eyewitness isn't reliable. It was dark and that leaves room for error."

"Miss Leroux, doesn't that put a dent on our case?" asked one of the associates."

"It could. That's the unfortunate thing. The car is the same make and model of the car Brandon drives. Still, that doesn't prove anything. The jury will have reasonable doubt. I don't believe they have a convincing case, but we shouldn't be overly confident either."

"Okay," he said.

"I'll be out of town next week. I know this isn't a great time, but I have a family issue."

She stretched the truth a bit, but it was a family issue because she needed to go see her sister and needed a break from all the stress going on in her life.

"Scott, I'll need you to go to the convenience store to interview people who frequent the area around there. See if they can tell you anything that will be useful for our defense..."

Suddenly, she stopped talking and began to feel dizzy.

"Miss Leroux, are you ok?" Sheila asked.

"Oh, I'm okay. I didn't eat breakfast this morning, so I'm sure that's it," she said with a smile.

"I know the footage from the cameras was quite grainy.

Were you able to take it to the video forensics department to clear it up?"

Tiffany cleared her throat and grabbed her chest. Her heart was palpitating and she was felt cold. She started to sweat, and her breathing became heavy.

"Umm…excuse me for a moment."

Everyone's eyes were on her as she hurried out of the conference room. Some asked if she was okay, but she couldn't stop to talk.

Running to her office, Tiffany flung open the door and ran to her desk. It felt like an 80-pound weight was on her chest and it was harder to breathe.

Suddenly, she fell out of her chair knocking everything on her desk to the floor. Hearing the commotion, Ana ran into her office.

"Oh my God!" Miss Leroux!"

Tiffany could hear Ana and the EMT's voice, but was in a place she'd never been in before. Her vision became blurry and she slowly closed her eyes. Her emotions were out of control and too much on her body. The panic attacks were happening too much. The two were related and she finally crashed.

~~~~~~

"You scared me to death!" Angela yelled.

Tiffany had been admitted to the hospital. Angela was listed as an emergency contact and she rushed to the hospital when she was called.

Tiffany gave her a weak smile.

"I'm okay now. The doctor said that I had a serious panic attack. They want me to stay overnight just to make sure that everything is okay."

Angela walked over to the hospital bed and took Tiffany's hand.

"Well, I'm staying with you then. I took the rest of the day off. And don't object because you got me out of work for the day." she said while laughing.

"Besides, I might snag one of these fine doctors!"

She gave Tiffany a high five

"Well, I expect a gift from you for getting you out of work then, silly."

Angela's eyes began to water.

"Seriously, I'm worried about you. You've got to take care of yourself," she said in a serious tone.

"He just broke my heart so bad. I almost wanted God to take me with him, but He told me to hold on, even if it's for you guys."

"Anderson is a jerk and is not worth your health Tiff. Don't even focus on him right now. I know you're hurting, but I just hope that you will realize that."

Tiffany lowered her head and said, "I know it, but it hurts so bad. I sit and think about him with that other woman. She's in my place now. I'm on the outside looking in...she has what I'm supposed to be having." Her voice trembled.

"What if they get married? What if she has his child? Why couldn't it be with me?"

She reached for the tissue and wiped her eyes as she cried. "Tiffany, I see where you're coming from, but you were with a selfish man who pretended to love you, all the while cheating. You could've found this out after you two got married and had kids. It could've been much more complicated and even more painful."

She sat down in the chair beside Tiffany's hospital bed.

"It'll take some time, I know, but just try to change your perspective just a bit. Trust God on this one."

Angela was right. The breakup shook her up so bad that she could only think about him and what they had.

"I appreciate the truth, Angie. I just gotta let it hit my heart."

"As long as you value yourself Tiff, it has."

"Enough about me. How are you feeling? Still nauseous?"

Angela rubbed her stomach and said, "Not as much. I found out that french fries from McDonald's help. It's not as bad as it was the other day."

Angie took Tiffany's hand.

"Now, I'm going to go get you some real food. That lunch tray looks disgusting. What do you want?"

"I'm not hungry right now, maybe later. I gotta call my parents back. I appreciate it though."

"Okay, I'll be right back. If you change your mind just call me."

"Will do."

~~~~~~

10 SECURITY

"Mommy, I promise you that I'm okay."

"Well, it's a good thing Angie called us. Tiff, you are not above needing our help. You'll always be our baby no matter how old you get. We're on our way right now."

"I've just been stressed and had not been sleeping and eating like I should, that's all."

She softened her voice. It wasn't her mother's fault, she was just concerned.

"Well, that will do it to you. You can't go around not eating or sleeping. No matter what's going on, your body needs rest. This is your body's way of telling you that."

"I know, I'll try to do better. I'm just so used to doing things on my own, you know?"

Tiffany was praying that her parents wouldn't come. She was exhausted and didn't have the energy for the company. Being alone was her only request.

"I know Tiff. You have to realize that you can't do it all. One day God will send you someone that will help you, but you will still need to rest no matter what. I know you're still dealing with the breakup, which doesn't help."

Her mother was right. Everyone was right. The common statement amongst everyone was that she was doing too much.

"Have you been keeping up with your therapy appointments?"

"No."

"You need to make an appointment with her as soon as possible. You're dealing with too much right now."

"I'll call her tomorrow mom."

"Okay. I'll let you get some rest and give you a call later tonight."

"Okay, mom. I love you."

"Love you too Tiff."

She went into the kitchen and filled her teapot with water. Thinking about the last few days, she couldn't believe what happened. The whole situation was embarrassing.

How much did her colleagues know? What if they felt that she wasn't fit to be partner?

The sound of the whistle from the teapot made her jump. She placed the chamomile tea bag in the teacup and headed over to her couch. Her cell phone rang and she dug into her bag to get it. It was Payton.

"Hello?" she tried not to sound too excited but was happy to hear his voice.

"Tiffany, it's Payton. I hope I'm not bothering you. I called your office and Ana said you were sick. Are you okay?"

She cleared her throat.

"Hey, I'm much better. I came home today."

"You sound tired. Do you need anything? Payton asked.

"Food, magazines, company?"

Tiffany hesitated.

"No, I don't need anything. It would be nice to see you though."

"Okay, I'm on the way. And I'm bringing an Essence magazine and some soup since Miss Independent is acting like she doesn't want anything."

Her stomach jumped. He was coming to her house, and she couldn't be happier.

"Thanks, Payton. I'll see you soon."

~~~~~~

Tiffany opened the door. Payton stood there with an Essence magazine and Panera Bread bag in the other hand.

"Excuse me, ma'am. Did you order a handsome man with food?"

Payton's greeting was hilarious and made her smile.

"Umm…can I come in?" Payton asked with a smile.

Tiffany came back from her trance.

"Of course, come on in."

Payton walked in and started to take off his sneakers.

"What are you doing?"

"I don't want to get your carpet dirty. I figured you might be one of those people."

"No, no. I don't care like that. Keep them on, please."

"Ok. I'll follow your orders, captain Leroux," he replied.

"Would you like anything to drink? Coffee? Water?"

Payton shook his head no as he walked towards the sofa.

"You're the one who should be sitting down. I brought you some chicken noodle soup and a magazine as promised."

He looked at the cover, which was graced with Idris Elba.

"Man, why do ya'll love this dude so much? He doesn't look better than me."

He had no idea that she thought he looked better than Idris Elba too. She was starting to master the art of keeping her thoughts about him to herself.

"Conceited much, sir?" Tiffany said with a smile.

He rubbed his mustache with both fingers

"Well, you know, what can I say?"

His imitation of J.J. from Good Times was hilarious.

Fixing his gaze on Tiffany he said, "And a certain someone has yet to sit down."

Tiffany sat down in the loveseat and became quiet.

"What going on Tiffany? Ana told me that you got sick, but I wanna know. Not in a professional way, but as a friend."

"Payton, I'd rather not…" Payton stopped her.

"Look, I understand why you're hesitant to tell me. I think that you're a smart, beautiful, strong woman, but you have to stop keeping everything in."

"I know. It's just hard for me to do. I don't know how to just let go."

"I just want to make sure you're okay lady. Not just saying it, but I mean it straight from the heart."

"I appreciate your concern and I will tell you this. I allowed a lot of situations to pile up on me. I wasn't taking care of myself as far as sleeping and eating and I just gave out."

Telling him the same thing she told her mother, just enough to address their concern and to keep him from going into the depressing details made her feel safe.

"Tiffany, I understand that you don't want to blur the lines, but you never know. Maybe I can help in some way."

She could feel his concern for her, so it was time to reveal more about her love life.

"I only told you a bit about how my relationship ended. I found out that he had been cheating through text messages. How long? I have no idea. He fell out of love with me."

Payton leaned forward and frowned, showing how he was paying attention to every detail.

"We were supposed to get married next spring, have a couple of kids, travel. You know, have a great life."

Once again, her voice shook, and she cleared her throat.

"So, with that, work, and everything else, responsibilities…it all came crashing down. I should have known better. I'm not a machine. I'm a human being and this "Strong Black Woman" mentality nearly killed me."

Silence.

"My mom was the same way, Tiffany. She looked out for everyone else, and after a while, it caught up with her. She began to have chest pains, constant headaches, and always had colds."

"Oh my goodness. Really?"

"Yep. The doctor told her that the stress was going to kill her. She had to lighten her load. I don't want that to happen to you." He looked away.

"My mom is my life, and I wouldn't have made it without her. She loves me unconditionally. Never missed a track meet, always there to help me with homework, cooked, tucked me in. All the while she was hurting."

"Wow. That must've been hard."

"Oh, it was. My dad stayed up many nights just watching her sleep. With her being so sick, it brought them closer together. All of us. I didn't want to leave Virginia to go to school because of how sick she was, but my mother told me not to put my life on hold for her."

Behind all of his jokes, it was evident that Payton had experienced hard times as well. It was as if he wasn't there with her as he told her about the situation.

Tiffany reached up and rubbed her scalp.

"Yea, my hair is falling out. I couldn't understand why my throat was always sore. The doctor told me the same thing when I was in the hospital. Sexy huh?"

"No, don't even think that way. The sexy thing about you right now is that you're opening up. Not a lot of people can talk like this."

"So, I also had a bad breakup before Anderson. I took so many emotional hits that my mother encouraged me to seek therapy. It was so embarrassing."

"Embarrassing? In what way?"

"Well, I felt like I was weak because I had to talk to someone. Why couldn't I work through it on my own?"

"So do you still go?"

"Yea. Haven't been in a while though. Do you think I'm weird?"

"No, I think you're strong. And I hope you will go see your therapist soon. It's no different than if you were physically ill."

Payton's acceptance of her made her heart swell.

Looking at her deep in the eyes, he said, "So stay true to your word because I don't want you to go anywhere."

"Scouts honor."

"I would like to stay and keep you company if that's okay,"

Payton said.

"I'm not trying to push up on you, let me make that clear. You look extremely bored, and I don't have any plans. Since you have Hulu, we can watch all the episodes of "The Boondocks.""

Instead, Tiffany went through her DVD collection.

"How about "Set It Off"?

"Cool! Just enough drama, action, and romance," Payton replied.

Tiffany shot him a serious look. "Relax Tiff. Just joking!"

"Besides, we aren't even sitting on the same couch," Payton said in a mischievous voice with a smirk.

"Come here," Payton said in a soft voice. Hesitant, Tiffany slowly walked over to the couch and sat beside him.

"Don't worry, I'm not gonna try anything. I just want you to know that you don't have to be guarded around me. Life is tough enough without having to carry a load. Is it okay if I hold your hand?"

"Yes, you can Payton."

11 REVELATION

"Hey, Lauren! I'm here!" Tiffany screamed into the phone.

"Yaaaaay!" I'll be there in about 15, can't wait to see you!"

Tiffany went outside and waited on the passenger pickup area after picking up her luggage from the baggage claim.

Looking down the row, she saw her sister's White Range Rover. She stood up and walked down the row of cars, so she wouldn't have to wait.

Lauren quickly exited her car and ran towards Tiffany. They hugged and loaded her luggage into her car.

"I can't believe you're finally here!"

"I know," Tiffany said.

"We're gonna have so much fun. Let real life go for a few days and paint the town." Lauren said while taking off.

As they headed down 21st street towards Lauren's condo,

Tiffany rolled down her window and let the air blow on her face. The sights and sounds of Manhattan excited her.

"You hungry?" Lauren asked.

"Yes. I don't eat a lot when I fly. Don't wanna be running back and forth to the restroom."

"Ok. Let's go to Patsy's,"

They ate at that restaurant the last time she visited, so Lauren knew that the food was delicious.

"Thank you," Tiffany and Lauren said as the waitress brought the food to the table.

"Yummy," Lauren said as the placed the napkin in her lap.

"So, I could tell something was wrong when you called me. You didn't sound like yourself. What's up?"

Tiffany pushed her food around on her plate.

"Lauren, I don't understand why my relationships turn out to be disasters. I've done all the right things. I made good grades, wasn't out in the streets, went to law school, and made partner. I'm supposed to be married with children. I treated Anderson like a king and thought that I would get the same in return. Our engagement is off. He was cheating."

Lauren's face showed both sympathy and anger while Tiffany told her the details of the story.

"Please don't tell me that I should've taken my time. We dated for three years so we knew each other very well, or so I thought."

Lauren bit her lip.

"Sis, you know me. I've been through some of the same situations. I just hate the fact that you're still having to deal with these jerks. I'm so sorry."

"I know."

Angela told her the same thing. She learned her lesson the hard way. Lauren continued.

"I remember when you both came to see me, and we went to see "Come Far Away." His phone lit up showing that he was getting texts and calls, one after the other. Almost as if the person calling wasn't going to stop until he answered. He's a piece of trash. Please!"

"I know. I let my desire for a man cause me to override

what I was feeling. That feeling that things were off. I mean, man, there were things done that I saw with both eyes. I excused them because I felt like I needed him."

Lauren shook her head.

"And because of that, he could do whatever he wanted to me. I own my part, I'm not putting all the blame on him. I shoulda ended it sooner."

"Tiff, that happens to a lot of women. Then the man moves on just like that."

"I know. I laid in bed the other night and looked back at my relationships, types of guys, my issues, mistakes. I don't have all the answers, but I know that I've got to find out, so it doesn't happen again. That's if there will be another chance to make better choices. I'm exhausted with men."

"I understand that. It's can be crazy out here, but don't give up hope."

Lauren paid for lunch and they walked out of the restaurant to the car. The skyscrapers were mesmerizing.

"Hey, Lauren. Do you ever stop to think about how your life would be different had you met someone else other than Chad?"

Chad Worden is a famous actor that Lauren had been dating for the past three years.

Lauren thought about it for a moment and said, "I do from time to time, but on the other hand I'm glad that I met Chad because he's so good for me. I love that I can be myself around him...goofiness and all. He makes me so happy."

"Well do you think that you could mess up God's plan for yourself? Like do you think spending time so much time with sorry guys kept me from meeting the right man?"

"Sis I know I'm not a preacher or anything, but I know that God wants us to experience the good and the bad. It could be that you just haven't met him yet."

This speech was irritating Tiffany. Hearing it repeatedly was getting old. Still, coming from Lauren felt a little different. She wasn't just saying words to dismiss her.

"Remember that scripture about trying not to figure everything out? Leaning on your understanding. I think I said it right." Lauren said with a slight frown.

Tiffany understood. She had to trust God's plan, no matter

how much it hurt.

~~~~~~

Tiffany opened her eyes and looked at the time on her cell phone. It was 9:00 at night. She smelled food and went downstairs.

"Well, hello sleepyhead sister."

"Hey, Lauren. I'm so sorry. I didn't mean to sleep for three hours."

"It's okay. I was about to wake you, but I figured with the jetlag and traveling you needed to rest. I'm cooking instead of us going out. You're here for a week, so we can go out tomorrow."

"I am. What are you cooking?

"Shrimp Scampy. Chad's gonna join us. He finished filming in New Orleans. He's been going back and forth for three months now, so we get some quality time."

"That's great! I haven't seen Chad in so long."

The doorbell rang, and Lauren quickly walked to her door. "Hey, Woobie!" Chad gave her a big hug.

"Chad you have a new nickname for me every time I see you."

Chad looked up and saw Tiffany sitting at the kitchen table. "Hey! Look who finally came into town!"

He walked up to Tiffany and hugged her.

"I know, I know. Lauren already gave me that lecture," she said, rolling her eyes.

"Dinner's ready!"

Lauren set the table and motioned for them to have a seat.

"So how have things been Tiff?" Chad asked.

"Busy, busy, busy. The practice keeps me so busy. I'm so glad to be here to rest for a few days."

"I feel you on that."

"Oh yeah, congrats on your Oscar."

"Thanks, Tiff. It's surreal, you know? All these years of hard work paid off."

"So proud of my baby," Lauren said smiling at Chad.

"Oh come on. Get a room you guys," Tiffany said.

"How's the wedding planning going? It's coming up next spring, right? I can't wait to meet him. Amazingly, our lives have been so crazy that I haven't even met your fiancé." Chad said while shaking his head.

Tiffany dreaded the question. And didn't quite know how to answer it.

"We broke up. I'm just trying to take it one day at a time."

"I get it. Do you mind if I ask what happened?

"Chad don't push her. It's a touchy subject."

"No Lauren, it's okay. It is what it is. I loved the great Anderson Owen so much. I didn't see it coming, but all I can try to do is move on. I encouraged him and loved him. But I guess what I did doesn't matter."

Chad frowned and said, "Tiffany, I hate to tell you this, but when I was working with him on "The Life of Man," we chatted for a while in his office." There were pictures of him with some girl. He said he's in a relationship and is planning to get married next year. Something like they've been together for a year."

Tiffany stopped chewing and let the fork drop to her plate.

~~~~~~

After hearing the information, she just knew that she would throw up all the food she'd eaten.

"I'm so sorry sis"

"No, it's okay," Tiffany said.

"This good thing is you know now just in case that clown tries to ease his way back in. You know me as your sweet sister, but when it comes to my loved ones, I don't play."

"I agree Tiffany," Chad said in an angry tone.

"He doesn't have to worry about me being all chummy. I had no idea he was such a jerk."

"Thanks, Chad."

Tiffany could feel herself blush from embarrassment.

"I'll be back." Tiffany quickly got up and headed towards the bathroom. She closed the door and stared at herself in the mirror.

"Don't cry. Don't cry" Tiffany whispered to herself.

"Hey, Lauren. Go check on her," Chad said.

"That was some heavy news she just heard. I'll be out here. You two talk as long as you need to."

Three soft knocks came from the other side of the door.

"Sis? Can I come in?"

The door slowly opened, and Lauren walked into the

bathroom

She didn't say anything, just reached out and hugged her.

"Lauren, I'm just so tired. I was down enough and then I find out that he's planning a life with another woman. I'm afraid I'm going to lose it."

After that, her words became inaudible. It didn't matter anyway; her words didn't mean anything. Neither did she.

11 RAGE, LOVE

"I'm gonna miss you Tiff. You'd better not let a year go by without coming to the NY!" Lauren said while playfully punching her in the shoulder.

The week she was there sped by and before she knew it, it was Saturday.

Tiffany assured her that she would make it a point to visit her more often.

"You call me as soon as you land, okay? And don't forget, were family and I'm always here. Call me at 2 am if you feel like it. I hate to see you hurting so much."

They said their goodbyes and Tiffany quickly walked away. She always hated goodbyes and preferred to keep it short as she tears up when leaving.

The announcement to board came over the loudspeaker, so she headed towards her gate.

Tiffany took a seat and listened to the safety procedures. She didn't like how the actors smiled robotically as they showed how to put on safety equipment.

The pilot announced "Flight attendants, prepare for take-off, please. Cabin crew, please take your seats for take-off."

After they cleared everyone to be able to use electronics, she once again put her headphones on and played some music. "The Lady in My Life" by Michael Jackson played. She realized that she keeps hearing this song. It must be because this is something she yearned for.

"I will keep you warm. Through the shadows of the night."

A tear fell down her cheek and she quickly changed the song.

There was no protection from the night for her. She closed her eyes and began to say a prayer. Her mind was so stuffy that she couldn't think of the words to say. She simply lowered her head and said in a whisper, "Lord, I need you!"

~~~~~~

"Here we go again," Tiffany whispered to herself.

She unlocked her door and looked around. It almost escaped her mind that she was supposed to call her sister when she got in. picking up the phone, she dialed Lauren's phone number.

"Hey! I'm back home!"

"Great!" Lisa said. "How was your flight?"

"It was okay. This lady kept trying to talk to me, so I put on my headphones. I miss you already."

"Hey, sis. You don't have to hide your pain from me. I know that you were already in pain and then information you got when you were here didn't help."

Tiffany could hear, the concern in her voice.

"You know you're welcome here anytime, okay?"

Tiffany replied, "Girl, I told you I'm fine! We both knew he's a jerk and that confirmed it."

"Alright, I'm gonna call you later. Pick up the phone or I'll keep calling you!"

Lisa was telling the truth. When she wanted to talk, she wanted to talk.

"Okie, dokie!"

"Love you Tiff."

"Love you too Lauren."

Tiffany grabbed her keys and headed out the door. She decided to do something that made her happy and sad.

~~~~~~

Neighborhoods had always seemed so warm to her. Beautiful homes, manicured lawns, lights inside, and garages were what she saw.

What were the families doing? Were they watching TV? Were they having dinner and arguing about which child would do the dishes?

She drove around Lake's Edge and saw a couple getting out of the car with groceries. The wife headed into the house, but the man went back and forth to take the groceries to the car. It's the little things like this that she wanted.

It was time to go back home. She had enough of looking at the happiness of others when she felt like she was behind in life. Jealousy wasn't an option. Everyone deserves happiness.

"Uggggh!" Tiffany screamed.

"Why is this light so long?"

The light finally turned green. Her car screeched as she took off and realized that she was taking her anger out on her car. She slowed down and pulled into her parking space.

As she opened the car door, a car with tented windows went by slowly in front of her house. It stopped and no one got out. She ran into the house, locking the door behind her.

"Oh my God," Tiffany said while leaning against the door.

Her cell phone was in her purse, and she dug into it trying to find it.

"911 What's your emergency?"

"Yes, there is a strange car sitting outside of my house. I'm at 755 Beacon Lane."

"Ok, ma'am. Are you able to see the make and model of the car?"

"No, I ran into my house. I couldn't see it. Can you please hurry?"

"Ma'am I've already dispatched the police. I'll stay on the phone until they arrive."

Tiffany looked through the blinds. The car was still there.

"Thank you."

~~~~~~

"We canvased the area, but we didn't find anyone. It could be some of these teenagers fooling around. We'll look around again, but please keep your door locked. If you see anything else suspicious, please call us back.   "

Tiffany spoke with tears in her eyes.

"I appreciate it, officer."

"You're welcome. Are you here alone?"

"Unfortunately yes."

"Is there anyone you can call to stay with you for a bit? I hope I'm not overstepping my bounds, but you look scared."

'Yes, I can call someone. Thanks for your concern."

"You're most certainly welcome. Don't forget, call if anything else looks weird."

"I sure will. Good night."

"Good night," he said with a smile.

Tiffany picked up her phone and started dialing frantically.

"Come on Angie."

Angie didn't pick up, so she dialed it again.

"Hello, you have reached Angie Sinron. I'm not available to take your call at this moment. Please leave your name, number, and a brief message. I will get back to you at my earliest convenience."

With her hands shaking, she ended the call. She didn't know who to call.

"Payton," she whispered.

There it was in her "recent" list. What would she say? Is it appropriate to call? She wondered how to call him without sounding desperate.

Biting her lip, she dialed his number. He picked up, but she couldn't speak.

"Hello? Tiffany?"

He said it again and she opened her mouth not knowing what was going to come out of it. It was best just to be honest. There was no room for pride.

"Hey, Payton. Somebody was sitting outside of my house and…" Tiffany was talking fast and suddenly, burst into tears. She managed to get a few words out.

"Can you please come over? I'm so scared."

"Of course! I'm leaving right now. What's your address?"

Protection. She'd never known what that felt like from a man. Knowing that she was scared caused him to immediately go into action. Protecting everyone in her life was such a habit that it was hard for her to receive it.

"Thank you so much Payton." Tiffany whispered in an exhausted voice.

~~~~~~

Hearing her doorbell ring made her jump. Tiffany slowly walked to the door and looked through the peephole. It was Payton.

She turned off the alarm and opened the door.

"What's going on Tiff?"

Tiffany threw her arms around him, still crying. He pulled away and looked deep into her eyes.

"Hey! I'm here now calm down. Tell me what's wrong."

"I don't know. There was a car outside of the house. It creeped me out. The windows were tinted, and it was going by real slow. All of a sudden it stopped."

"Really?"

"Yes. I called the police, but they didn't see anybody. That scares me even more."

"Okay, that was the right move. That and calling me."

"Yea. I've never been afraid of being here alone, but I was terrified. Thank you for coming over."

He lead her over to the couch and sat beside her. Her head was hanging down and he slowly lifted it.

Tiffany didn't know where to look, so she looked back down. Payton slowly lift his hand and wiped away her tears.

"I'm just so tired, Payton."

"Look, nothing is going to happen to you. I'm here, okay?"

"Okay."

"Do you want me to stay the night with you?"

"Yes, please stay," Tiffany whispered.

"I'm too scared to go to sleep."

"Well, hopefully, you will be a little more at ease with me here."

He gently pulled her up from the couch.

"Hey, why don't I make you some tea. Go take a shower and relax. I'm right here, so you can feel at ease.

"Ok. I'll be right back."

As Tiffany walked into the bathroom, Payton followed her Tiffany looked at him in shock. She thought that he was there to help her, not to take advantage of her.

He walked to the bathtub and turned on the water.

"I don't want you to have to lift a finger right now. Let me prepare it for you."

"Payton, you don't have to do that."

"Look, a lot has been going on. All I want you to do is let me take care of you for a while."

He walked over to the linen closet to get a towel.

"I know exactly what you're thinking. I don't want anything other than for you to feel safe, so take a nice long bath to calm yourself down. I'll be in the living room."

"I know, but I'm just used to guys wanting to go too fast, that's all."

For the first time in weeks, she felt a bit of happiness. There was someone there to help her, to protect her. After her bath, she put on her pajamas and walked into the living room.

"Hey! I thought you got lost!" Payton yelled.

"I see you got jokes. Nah, I'm so refreshed right now. I feel relaxed.

"Come here," He said it in such a gentle way that she couldn't resist the offer. She walked over to the couch, sat down, and laid her head on his shoulder.

12 PAYTON

Tiffany woke up to find herself asleep on the couch. She wondered why she smelled breakfast. Sitting up slowly she saw Payton in the kitchen cooking.

"This has to be a dream," she thought.

Squinting her eyes, she realized that he was there. She walked into the kitchen and there was Payton making breakfast.

"Good mornting. You hungry?" Payton said.

"And yes, I meant to put the "t" in it. Madea is my aunt."

Tiffany rolled her eyes.

"Oh, come on. Just joking. You had such a hard night last night, so I figured that you would like to breakfast. I was going to ask you if you wanted to go out but figured you'd rather eat here. I hope you don't mind me cooking"

Tiffany let out a yawn.

"Yea, it's ok. Thanks for making breakfast."

"So, missy, what's on the agenda today?"

'I'm not sure. Still tired."

"I was wondering if you would like to go out later…maybe to the park. Get some fresh air." Payton said.

"I have a ton of work to do, so that'll be it. Gotta prep for this case, it won't win itself."

She wanted to spend the day with him but was a ball of confusion. Maybe it wouldn't hurt. Her mind was too jumbled to work anyway.

"On the other hand, I guess I could go out for a bit. Get my mind off things until I figure out what to do."

"Great. How about Lafitte.?" Payton suggested.

"That sounds great."

"Okay beautiful. Go get ready. It's gonna be a good day."

"So, Ms. Leroux, I guess you want to know more about me," Payton said as they strolled in the park.

"Yeah, I'm curious to know more. We've been so focused on me that I don't even know that much about you."

"Well, I'm originally from Chesapeake, Virginia. My parents decided to move there when I was in middle school. I have two sisters, one older, and one younger. Didn't like it here at first because I loved the beach in Virginia, but I've come to love nature here."

Payton went on with the details of his life.

"I went to New Orleans University. Majored in engineering. A bit of a nerd. I'm not that interesting."

They both laughed looking down as they walked.

"I've never been married but hope to be someday. Right now, I just hope to meet the right person. My parents have been married for 50 years."

"I agree. Marriage is serious. Gotta make sure you know them. That's so beautiful to hear how your parents have been together for so long," Tiffany said.

"Yea. You don't see that these days. As soon as trouble or hard times happen, marriages end. It's like people forget about the "for better or worse" part of the vow. Sad."

"It is", Tiffany said.

"So, since I grew up with that as an example, I always wanted that for myself. I want a good woman in my life. Our love would be mutual. We would be a team."

Tiffany always wanted that for herself but was hesitant to tell him. Every time she gets excited, things go bad. She decided to keep it to herself.

"So, other than you being an attorney, I don't know much else about you. I'm not trying to pry, I just know that there is more to you than your career and Anderson." Payton said in a soft voice.

"Well. I'm originally from here. My parents have been married for 40 years. I have one sister who lives in NY. I went to college at Loyola University and my major was pre-law. I graduated from Law School there."

"Oh okay."

"I graduated first in my class from law school. I don't like pets, favorite color is blue, and I love banana pudding. Anything else?" Tiffany said with a laugh.

"Well dag! That was a quick rundown!"

She gave him a playful push and they kept strolling down the marsh.

"Forty years! Wow! So, like me, you know what it's like to see a marriage that lasts. That's rare these days. I'm sure your parents have a lot of memories. It's wonderful to grow with a person throughout life. You know, see each other mature. I can't imagine."

Her hopes and dreams were in his words

"I know. I've always admired how my parents were able to stay together through thick and thin."

"I bet you are."

"You know Payton. I just knew that was going to be me. That was supposed to be the order in my life. Graduate from college, go to law school, get married, and have a girl and a boy."

"The perfect life," Payton said.

"Maybe I was too picky throughout my 20's. That's when a lot of people get engaged and married. Then there's my biological clock."

Payton stopped and looked Tiffany in her eyes.

"Tiff, please stop being so hard on yourself. You have accomplished so much in life. More than many people can say they have."

"Yea," Tiffany said softly. "It's funny, I had plans, but I was always with a man that didn't treat me right. As much as I wanted that life, I didn't want to go into a marriage or have a child with someone who treated me so badly. In the end, I just didn't get lucky enough to meet the right one."

She quickly wiped her eyes and hoped it was the last tear that would fall in front of him. Payton didn't see it. She held her head down as they were walking, so she was able to wipe them away. Suddenly, she felt a sense of panic.

"You know what Payton. I can't do this."

She turned and walked away, and he quickly grabbed her hand.

"Tiffany! What's wrong? Did I do or say something to upset you?"

He seemed genuinely concerned, but that did nothing for the knot in her stomach.

"You don't get it, Payton. I can't open myself. The only thing there is confusion and pain. I'm safe where I am right now. I only have to deal with me, not someone wreaking havoc on the grains of peace I have left."

Payton opened his mouth to speak, but nothing came out. There was nothing to say, he knew that Tiffany was speaking from the heart.

"Okay, I understand. I'm sorry."

That was the best thing Payton could say to her No lectures, no judgments. Just that he understood where she was coming from.

"Thank you. I just need you to hear me."

Payton nodded his head.

"I think we should head back to your house. Maybe you need a breather."

"I'm sorry Payton. I'm just so tired of the ups and downs and back and forth. I just want to be happy."

She felt a gentle hand on her shoulder. Payton turned her around.

"You don't have to explain. I get it" he said.

"Let's do dinner tonight Tiffany. I'm enjoying spending this day with you and I don't want it to end. I'm not going to take anything from you. I just want to be around you."

Payton lit a fire in her that was beyond all the pain she was experiencing.

I'll take you home so that you don't get tired of me, and I can pick you up around 8:00. We can go to Mulate's".

Mulate's was Anderson's favorite restaurant. Nevertheless, she agreed to go.

~~~~~~

"Yes, I would like a Sprite please," Tiffany said.

Payton looked up from the menu.

"And I'll have a sweet tea with lemon."

The waiter took the drink orders and walked away.

"Thank you, Payton. This is a nice treat. I want to apologize for earlier. It was rude of me and…"

Payton stopped her.

"Hey, don't apologize for your feelings, at least not with me. I have two sisters, so I get it. Ya'll go through some things with men. I need you to do me a favor though. Just relax and enjoy the moment, okay.?"

The waiter returned to the table.

"Are you two ready to order?"

"Yes, I would like the Crawfish Etoufee."

"Yes, ma'am. And you sir?"

"Let me get the Mulate's Jambalaya."

"Okay. Will there be anything else for you two? Perhaps an appetizer?"

"No we're good," Payton responded.

"Okay, great. I'll get your order right out to you."

Payton thanked the waiter and looked at Tiffany.

"How are you feeling?" he asked.

"Better, thanks to you. I'm so grateful that you were there for me. That you're a part of my..."

Tiffany's jaw dropped. She couldn't believe her eyes. It was Anderson. He was coming from the restroom and walking towards his table. She slumped down in her seat...

Anderson and his date got up to leave but Tiffany couldn't see her.

"Ummm...I'm going to the restroom, I'll be right back."

"Everything okay?"

"Yes. It's just that this Sprite is going through me."

Tiffany got up from the table in a hurry.

Payton turned his head to see where she was going, and he noticed that she walked past the bathroom towards the exit. Surprised, he waited a minute and realized that she wasn't coming back.

"Mr. Baptiste, would you like any more sweet tea? Sir? Sir?"

Payton came back from his trance.

"No, that'll be all. We have an emergency and must leave. I'm sorry. Here's the cost of the meal and you can keep the change."

The waiter looked shocked but wished him a good evening.

"Thank you, sir. This is the best tip I've ever had!"

Payton jumped up and couldn't walk fast enough. He ran outside and saw her walking quickly pass the valet towards a couple.

Tiffany stopped and yelled out "Anderson!"

Anderson turned around with a shocked look on his face. Then, the lady he was with turned around. It was Angie

14 TRUE COLORS

"Wha..."

Tiffany couldn't even get the word out. She couldn't breathe and was starting to feel dizzy.

Payton ran up behind her and said, "Tiffany. What are you

doing?"

"Anderson, what is going on? And Angie?"

"Hey Tiffany," Angie replied.

Tiffany couldn't believe how calm Angie was acting.

"So it was you all along? It was you and not somebody named Erica?"

"Yes, Tiffany. It just happened. You were always so busy, always neglecting him."

"I never neglected Anderson. I always supported and loved him."

"See that's the thing, Tiffany. You thought you were but it was the little things. They end up becoming big things."

"What "things" are you talking about Angie? Tiffany asked.

"Like one time he brought you lunch and you couldn't get off the phone long enough to eat it with him. Or the time when he wanted affection, but all you wanted to do was go to sleep."

Tiffany looked down at Angie's stomach.

"And the baby?"

"Yep, it's his."

"So all of this "he ain't nothing" talk was just a lie? You wanted him for yourself?"

"Yes.

Tiffany choked up.

"He made me smile every time I looked at him. He always smiled back, and this was right in front of you, but you were too preoccupied with work to notice it. Heck, you couldn't even put down a paper long enough to have a conversation!"

Angie still had that grin on her face. It was igniting furry in Tiffany and she didn't know how much more she could take. She squeezed her hands as she wanted to run up and choke both of them.

"You walk around like you're Miss Independent when you're the weakest woman I know. You don't know how to truly love a man. I'm so sorry but I'm doing the job you failed at."

Tiffany's heart began to race. Her stomach cramped up and she felt as if she was going to throw up. This revelation sickened her. For some reason, she looked at Anderson as if she expected him to back her up. He just stood there with the same grin on his face.

Angie shook her head at her and walked up to Tiffany.

"Don't go glaring at him. This is all your fault for taking him for granted. He was good for you, but you still wanted more."

"I never took him for granted, Angie."

"Well, that's what you think. You wanted it all but look at you now. I had to sit there and hear you complain when you had everything. I wanted what you had, so I could treat him better. Heck, I wanted him from day one."

She turned around and walked back to Anderson, grabbing his hand.

"Anderson, I gave you everything. When your mom died I was the one who gave you a shoulder to cry on. I was the one fixing soup when you had the flu. I didn't judge you when it took time for you to find directing projects and you could barely pay your bills. I was always supportive, and this is what I get?"

His face began to soften as if the words started to sink in.

"Did she do this for you? Or did she just lay on her back?"

"I'm so sorry, but Angie's ready to go. Her feet start to hurt if she stands too long."

Angie looked at Tiffany and rubbed her stomach.

They start to walk away, and Tiffany began to walk quickly towards them. Payton ran up behind her and grabbed her arm. Her legs collapsed, and she started screaming and crying. Payton grabbed her right before she completely hit the ground.

"Tiffany! Going after them isn't going to solve anything. Let's go." he whispered in her ear.

She was still screaming and crying.

"It's not fair! That was supposed to be me!"

Payton grabbed her and ushered her towards the valet.

"Yes, take me home! I don't need to be here with you. Y'all are all the same! Just words and deceit, never any honesty."

"Tiffany. You can't blame me for him being a jerk!"

His voice had a hint of anger, but she knew why. He wasn't Anderson or any other man for that matter.

Payton opened the passenger door for her and she quickly got in and slammed the door shut. He looked out of the window and turned towards her.

"Tiffany, I know he hurt you. I saw it first-hand. But please don't do this. Let me be here for you."

Looking at him with glaring eyes, she replied, "I said to take me home."

13 Truth

Three months later...

Tiffany walked into her office building. She took a deep breath when she walked towards her office

"Good morning Ms. Leroux."

Anthony was a newly hired paralegal. She wondered why he was there.

"Hi, Todd. What's going on?"

"Umm, Ana called this morning and said she wasn't coming in. She left us in a bind. I'm being trained myself and I gotta stop for this."

He shook his head. Tiffany could see the frustration in his face. She remembered those days of working hard trying to make partner and couldn't imagine being a paralegal and stuck working as a secretary.

"Okay Todd, just hold on. I'll handle it."

"It's a pleasure working with you Ms. Leroux. That's what makes this a little easier. Most associates wouldn't care, so I appreciate it."

"No problem, I promise I'll fix it. I have a meeting with a client and his uncle at 11:00, so I'll be in my office preparing for the meeting."

"Sure thing Ms. Leroux."

~~~~~~

Brandon and Payton arrived at her office. Tiffany motioned for them to sit down.

"How are you to doing today?" she said while shuffling through papers.

It was awkward seeing him since the dramatic scene at the restaurant.

Either way, she had a job to do and was true to her word about representing Brandon to the best of her abilities.

Taking a deep breath, she looked Brandon in the eyes.

"Look, I'm going, to be honest with you. Things don't look good as of right now. My team is working hard to maintain your innocence. Unfortunately, your friend Chase was arrested and turned state's evidence to avoid being convicted of this charge. He pointed his finger at you and named you as the ring leader."

"Huh? He's lying, man."

"After looking at the tape and questioning witnesses, Chase was identified and arrested at home a week after the robbery. He said he was with you, and you can't prove where you were. I know you said that he was with you Payton, but this doesn't look good. Is there something you want to tell me? I can't defend you with limited information. I need honesty, now."

Brandon rolled his eyes and took a deep breath.

"Look, I told you that I wasn't there. What more do you need?"

He sat back and took out his phone. Payton noticed that he went to Instagram and became furious.

"There's a list of the evidence that DA Linwood will present at the trial. Let's look through the list and try to refute each one." Tiffany realized that one of the pages of the report was missing. She stood up and headed towards the door.

"I'll be right back. I have to get some material from my secretary's desk."

She walked up the hallway to the desk where Todd was working.

"Hey, Todd. I need you to print out the entire report showing the prosecution's evidence. It's saying three out of four. I don't have the last sheet."

He looked up at her trying to soften his expression.

"Here it is, it was mixed up with her paperwork."

"Well, I care, and I'll handle it for you"

After showing Todd appreciation, she headed towards her office. Stopping at the door, she heard what sounded like an argument between Payton and Brandon. They were trying to keep it down, but she could still hear the conversation.

"Look, Brandon, you are so ungrateful. Is Instagram more important than this case? We can't afford for you to be immature."

Tiffany could tell that Payton was gritting his teeth.

"I'm already paying to get you the best attorney. You were too busy hanging out with your no-good friends and you were raised better than that. If you had listened to your mother and me, none of this would've happened."

"Okay, okay Uncle P. I get it. I'm not supposed to have a life according to ya'll," Brandon said.

He shot Brandon an angry look.

"Keep your voice down."

"Alright."

"Not many people would be willing to lie for you. If it weren't for the promise I made to take care of you and your mother, I would've thrown you out to the wolves. But no, I'm lying to a beautiful woman who is working hard for us."

"Okay, okay. I get it, you care for her. I mean, she nice and all, but it doesn't seem like she's that great of any attorney. The only thing she ever says is that things don't look good. Blah, blah, blah."

"I'm going to the restroom. When she comes back you'd better not have that disrespectful attitude."

He walked towards the door and opened it, still angrily looking at Bandon. When he opened it and turned to the left, Tiffany was standing there. Payton had a look of shock on his face.

"Tiffany, let me explain, please. I..."

Tiffany glared at him and tried to keep her voice quiet as some of her colleagues were walking past them.

"I'm going to keep this as quiet as possible. I need you to get the heck out of my office. Now."

It was the same situation as when she caught Anderson on the phone in the restaurant.

The hurt she felt in her face was indescribable. Trembling from anger, she even scared herself.

Payton was quiet. It seemed as if he was trying to figure out what to say. He was caught. There was no explanation and he knew that.

"Tiffany, please. Can we please sit down and talk? I wanted to tell you, but things kept going and before I realized it..." He took a deep breath and his eyes teared up.

"Before I realized it, I was in love with you. These weeks of only talking to you about the case are so hard for me to do. I haven't talked to you or been around you. I didn't intend for us to meet and fall in love.

Tiffany's heart almost leaped out of her chest. She loved him and was afraid to tell him. Yet, he already knew how she felt.

"I said to get out of my office, you and your disrespectful imbecile of a nephew."

"Okay, if that's what you want I will leave."

Keeping his eyes on Tiffany, he slowly turned around.

"Brian let's go."

Brian was preoccupied with his phone and didn't hear him. "Brian!"

He looked up from his phone and said, "Huh?"

"I told you that we are leaving"

They walked out of her office and she'd never felt so empty. Taking a seat, she simply stared into space. It was true, love was not for her. After so many heartaches in the past, the same situation was happening again.

The laptop screen went dark allowing her to see her reflection. Tiffany realized that she would always be in the dark about love. She picked up her cell phone.

"Daddy, I'm gonna come home for a few days."

She needed a break from life, and the only way she could do that was to disconnect from her environment.

"Everything okay?"

"Yea, It's just that I haven't seen you guys in a while. I'll leave tomorrow after work."

"Can't wait to see you, baby girl! I'll let your mom know you'll be here!"

"Okay, I'll see you soon."

It was Friday and Tiffany was thrilled to go home and pack her bags to head home for a change of scenery.

"Phone, medicine, wallet, charger."

Tiffany made a mental note of necessities.

She grabbed her bags and headed to the car.

"Darn it!"

Tiffany was irritated as she tried to put her CD in and it dropped on the floor. There was a high likelihood that it was scratched. With the drive being an hour and a half, some good music was crucial.

She put in her Jill Scott CD and chose a song to listen to.

"Lighthouse" was the song that touched her heart.

"I am your shelter you're safe from harm. Tornado, lighting, hurricane…lay your burdens down."

~~~~~~

"Hey, daddy!"

Tiffany finally arrived at her parent's house. Her father was working on his car in the garage when she pulled up. Wiping his hands on a towel, he headed towards her car.

She grabbed her bags from the car and walked towards the house.

"No, no. I've got it. You go into the house," he said taking the suitcase out of her hand.

"Thanks, daddy. Did mama cook?"

He chuckled and said, "Is the sun hot? Go on in and get some of your mother's good cooking."

"Hey, mama!"

She hugged her mother as she walked into the living room.

"You hungry?"

"You know I'm always hungry for your cooking mom."

"I made lasagna. Homemade of course. Tiff, you know how I am. Just sit down and rest. I'll let you know when it's ready."

Her favorite recliner was calling her name. Before she turned to walk into the kitchen, her mother stopped her.

"You okay? You look tired"

"Mom, I'm okay. It's that I didn't get much sleep."

"I know you've been going through sweetie. How's it going?"

"I'm just so disappointed mom. We were supposed to be making wedding plans. I always envisioned you standing behind me, putting on my veil."

"Tiffany stop talking about your life as if these things won't happen. I'm glad this happened."

"Glad, why would you say that?"

"Because I never had a good feeling about him. It seemed as if he was always flirting or staring at women at different events he's been too. There was the family reunion, the Historical Law banquet he came to with you. Just didn't feel right."

"Mama, you were right. He cheated."

She walked over to Tiffany and hugged her.

"Look at me. It's by God's grace that you found out before walking down the aisle."

"I know mom."

"Let's eat, huh?"

"I'm gonna go outside and sit on the porch for a while. I miss this calm environment."

Her father walked around to the front of the house.

"Finally finished changing the oil in your mother's car. Your mother doesn't believe in keeping it up."

"Hey! I didn't hear you coming," Tiffany said with a smile. He walked up the steps and sat beside her.

"It's time for us to talk. Now I know you're going to pretend to be okay, but I won't accept that. I want you to tell me exactly what is taking the light out of you. I know the breakup was difficult, but there's something deeper than that."

The sounds of nature soothed her, and she knew that she had to come completely clean about her difficulties.

"Daddy, I don't get it. I mean, there are women younger than me that are married with children. What's wrong with me? Surely I would've been with someone if I was normal."

She tried to hold back her tears, but she decided to let them fall this time.

"Look, don't you go around thinking that. You have done so much in life. I don't mean just school or material things. Love and dedication are what people get when they have you in their lives."

"Why does everyone say that? I've heard that all my life, and now, I just don't believe it. I feel like I'm left out of life. There are things I won't ever experience. Kids, being a grandma, things like that."

"Stop that right now. You're not single because God doesn't love you. You're single because He does love you. These no-good men don't deserve you in any way. Sure, being with a man is easy, but if you want to be with a good man, trust God on that."

"I know daddy, but what about children? I'm 36 now, too old to carry a baby. What if I get with a man who wants children?"

He looked up at the sky.

"Stop looking at the water and look at Jesus. Trying to figure out when and where will only stress you out. The Lord has worked miracles in the past, now, and in the future. Don't go on thinking that He doesn't care about you."

Tiffany's tears kept falling. She knew that her father was right but just couldn't make her heart feel it right now. There were too many problems and she's taken too many hits to be able to believe. Maybe tomorrow, but not today.

"Hey, ya'll! Dinner's ready!" Her mom said.

Her dad patted her on the shoulder.

"Let's go get something to eat."

~~~~~~

Since the situation in Tiffany's office, her phone was ringing off the hook. Payton was calling back to back, but her heart wouldn't let her pick up the phone.

She decided to take a nap. Her phone rang, and she picked it up in her sleep.

"Tiffany. Hey, I know you don't want to talk to me, but please let me just say my part and I'll leave you alone. I owe you an explanation."

"Yes, you do, but I just can't do this with you, Payton. I should've known that something would happen eventually."

"Tiffany, other than for Brandon's case, I haven't talked to you personally in over a month. I miss you, I miss us."

Tiffany thought for a moment. Yes, she was hurt, but he needed to explain himself.

"Okay."

Payton let out a sigh of relief. "Can you meet me at Lafitte?

"I'll be back in town tomorrow. I can see you then."

"Ok, great. When you get back into town, give me a call."

"I will, and I want to make it clear that I'm meeting you to get an explanation. That's all."

14 EXCUSES

Payton looked so handsome when he stepped out of his car. He had on that black Puma baseball cap she loved on him, and a brown leather jacket. He walked up to her window.

"Hey, Tiff."

"Hey, Payton."

Payton reached out his hand to assist her.

"I can do it myself," Tiffany said

She grabbed her purse from the passenger seat and stepped out of the car.

They walked in silence for a while, then Payton motioned for them to sit on a bench.

"Tiffany please look at me."

"What is it, Mr. Baptiste? Why are we here?"

Her face was hard and cold.

"So, this is where we are? Going backward? Come on."

"I don't think you realize how much I hurt right now. Not only did you lie to me, you wasted my time and the time of my legal team. The rug has been pulled out from under me. I don't feel like the ground is stable. All I can do is cry because I thought you were different."

"I..."

"Exactly, you can't explain yourself. Well, let me explain this. I'm not taking on your case. You won't even get a referral from me. All I need you to do is leave me alone. Let me go and pick up the pieces of life again."

She wiped the tears from her eyes. Payton took her hands.

"Do you realize how hard I was working for Brandon? How I sat up at night thinking about strategies to present to my team?" "Tiffany, I don't expect you to do anything else for me. If anything, I need to be making up for your heart being broken again. I decided not to enable Brian anymore. His mother found

94

another attorney because she feels as if he can do no wrong. I didn't want to argue with her about how her son makes bad decisions and doesn't think about others.

"Oh really?"

"Yea. Since this was the first time he's been in trouble, they gave him probation for a year."

"Good for him," Tiffany said.

"I realized that I did the best that I could, but he had to save himself. He's not the only one being punished though. I lost the only person that meant the world to me. You."

His words struck a chord. Deep down she knew that he didn't mean to hurt her, he just put family first. Still, how was she ever going to trust him again?

"I can't do this," she said softly

"My heart can't do this. It will stop beating if I put it out there again Payton. Just when I started to trust again, I got knocked down."

Tiffany let out a laugh as she cried.

"Joke's on you Tiff. Love is for everyone but you."

"Tiffany please don't say that. Wait a minute, did you say the word love? Were you in love with me?"

"I gotta go."

"Tiff! Please talk to me!"

"Again, it's Ms. Leroux. You don't have the right to call me Tiff anymore."

She quickly walked to her car. Opening the car door, she got in and started up the car. As she was driving away, she glanced in her rearview mirror and caught a glimpse of him still standing there. It made perfect sense. He was behind her, in her past now. It cut her heart like a knife.

15 CHANCE

Two weeks later...Tiffany went to Holly Beach and walked along the shore. The breeze from the ocean was refreshing. It would be nice to have a peaceful life like the ocean. As the breeze went across her face, she started to smell the faint scent of cologne

She knew his scent, it was unique to him, and soothed her. She felt a hand on her shoulder and turned around. It was Payton.

"How did you know I was here? Have you been stalking me?"

"Your father told me. Please don't be mad at him. We had a long talk and he gave it to me straight. He said you were not put on this earth to be lied to. You are to be protected from the beginning to the end."

Rolling her eyes, Tiffany replied, "Well that's good, but I didn't come here to look at you. I came here to get some peace. Two things you took from me."

She walked away quickly, stomping through the sand. It didn't matter to her anymore. It didn't bother her that people were regretful or sorry. There were enough apologies to last her for the rest of her life.

"Tiffany! Please come back."

She returned to her hotel room at the Ritz Carlton and called her father.

"Daddy, why did you tell Payton where I was? I have nothing to say to him. I just want to be by myself at the beach for a couple of days."

"Sweetie, before you lose it, I need to talk to you. I was afraid to tell you this because you feel like you can't trust anyone. When your mom and I got married, I had an affair."

Tiffany's heart dropped.

"What. How could you daddy? I thought that you were the

only man in my life that I can trust."

"Baby girl, I was young and stupid. Your mom and I had been married for three years. I was 23 and your mom was 22. We went through the fire because of my dumb decision. We talked about it, even had to go to counseling. Over time, your mother learned to trust me again. Good people make stupid decisions, but don't give up."

If she heard any more shocking news, she swore that her heart would stop beating.

"I know you love him. You don't want to admit it, but you do. When he called me, I could hear his pain too. Now I told him that I would make his life difficult if you decide to take him back and he doesn't do right by you. It's entirely up you take him back, it's entirely up to you. I do know that you two love each other. Just think about it."

"Daddy I gotta go."

Tiffany hung up the phone and walked out on the balcony. She threw her head back and looked up at the sky. If only she could be with God right now, she wouldn't have to feel any more pain. It's not that she wanted to die, she just didn't want a life where she always looking from the outside in. Wanting so much to be happy, normal, and hopeful.

"Forgive. Love."

Those words came to her along with a warmth that covered her. God wanted her to forgive Payton.

"But God, it's not fair," she whispered.

She could still hear those words. The voice was soft, yet strong.

Tiffany slowly brought her head down and looked forward. It was time to go back to the shore where she wanted to be.

As she went back to the shore, she saw a man standing there at a distance. It was Payton. He walked towards her, but she stood in her place.

It amazed her that he was still there. He reached out to hold her, and she pulled back.

He slowly took both of her hands and held them to his chest.

"My heart beats for you."

Tiffany turned her head away and stepped back.

"I know Tiff. It's all my fault. My selfishness and deceit

destroyed us. I beat myself up about it every day."

"I'm just so scared, Payton."

"I was about to leave when I heard a voice tell me I can't leave you. Even though I've caused you so much pain, it was my job to help you heal and protect you," Brandon replied softly.

She turned around and all she could do was close her eyes.

"Payton, I said that I..."

"Let me make it up to you every day for the rest of our lives."
He stepped closer to her and held her close.

"I'm not going anywhere."

"You promise?"

"Yes, when I met you, I dreamed about you every night. In the dream, we would be together everything would be fine. All of a sudden, you'd turn into water. Everything in your life was okay, but then they would fall apart. Now I know that I was the cause of it this time. I made God and your father a promise that I would do whatever it takes to keep you."

Payton looked her in her eyes, once again revealing so much that Tiffany could barely hold his gaze.

"When I talked to my mother about what happened, she also said that I was wrong. I was told that I'd better hope that you forgive me, but she understands if you don't. My biggest fear is that I made a choice that will cause me to lose you. That God had a plan for me to be with you, but now, that chance is gone."

These words truly touched her because she felt the same way. She assumed that she'd messed up her life. Now, God is showing her that she wouldn't lose him because she made some poor decisions with men. He showed her grace and still sent a good man to her.

"Lord I'm gonna need your help with this," Tiffany thought to herself.

"Okay. I'll need your help and patience with this Payton. I'm hurt, but that pain doesn't take away my love for you."

Payton smiled that smile that always melted her heart, dimples and all.

"Thank you for forgiving me. Well, for taking the time to start this journey of forgiveness for us. I'll cherish you every day of my life."

A flash of all the times that she asked God for forgiveness ran quickly across her mind. This time, she would have to extend the same forgiveness to him.

Payton took her hand and lead her closer to the shore. They both stared into the ocean without saying a word.

Tiffany was no longer worried about her dreams slipping through her hands like water. It was her fears that needed to fall out of her hands, leaving room for happiness.

"I love you, Payton."

"I love you too Tiffany."